# GIRL ON A BICYCLE

First published in 1977 by
The Irish Writers Co-operative
This edition 2009 by
Liberties Press
Guinness Enterprise Centre | Taylor's Lane | Dublin 8
www.LibertiesPress.com | info@libertiespress.com | +353 (1) 415 1224
Trade enquiries to CMD BookSource
Tel: +353 (1) 294 2560
Fax: +353 (1) 294 2564

Distributed in the United States by
Dufour Editions
PO Box 7 | Chester Springs | Pennsylvania | 19425

and in Australia by
James Bennett Pty Limited | InBooks
3 Narabang Way | Belrose NSW 2085

ISBN: 978–1–905483–79–2

2 4 6 8 10 9 7 5 3 1

A CIP record for this title is available from the British Library

Liberties Press gratefully acknowledges the financial assistance of the Arts
Council in relation to the publication of this title.

Cover design by Ros Murphy
Internal design by Liberties Press
Printed by ColourBooks | 105 Baldoyle Industrial Estate | Dublin 13

# GIRL ON A BICYCLE

## LELAND BARDWELL

For Jacqueline

# PART I

# 1

One early morning in May I was running down Lansdowne Road in the direction of the RDS.

As I wheeled into Merrion Road, I had to wedge in and out between superbly manicured horses, well-turned-out boys and girls, middle-aged women with high chins and coloured scarves; I floundered amongst a flock of sheep that was holding up the traffic and avoided a magnificent Hereford bull who was being hauled along on his nose-ring by a farmer in a serge suit and wellington boots.

At the corner of Anglesea Road I caught sight of my sister, Columbine, travelling along in her mercurial fashion, carrying bridles, head collars, martingales and a sack full of cleaning gear.

'Where were you, last night?' she said.

'Was the da raging?'

'Why didn't you phone?'

'I forgot.'

'You forgot,' she said, hurrying on. 'You forgot. Tell that to the marines.'

'Well. So what?'

'We were worried stiff. The da was fuming.'

'Very sorry.'

'Well where, anyway?'

'I was with Nicholas and Nancy. I stayed at Nancy's house.'

'All very respectable,' said Columbine, sarcastic.

'Nicholas asked me to go to the theatre.'

'Asked you?'

'And why not?'

She regarded my baggy cotton shirt and the gap between it and my men's flannel trousers, which were rolled at the hems.

'Amazing. And did you go?'

'No.'

'What did you do?'

'Had a bath. Got drunk.'

'Had a bath?'

'Yes,' I said, patient. 'Nicholas made me take a bath.'

'Are you all right?'

'Yes. And here endeth the cathechism,' I said.

I snatched one of her bundles, saying: 'Allow me.'

'Don't bother,' Columbine said, snatching it back.

At the Anglesea Gate, we faced each other in cold hostility. 'Did you or didn't you?' she said.

I didn't reply.

Columbine started up again. 'We have to plait the manes. You were supposed to exercise Furioso yesterday. Why didn't you?'

'You didn't make it clear.'

'You must have been very busy not to use your loaf.'

'I was.'

'And did you?'

'No. Now are you happy?'

Columbine smiled.

We passed through the gate into the familiar puritan smell of horse dung and leather. When we reached the stables, I picked up two wooden buckets and, going to the tap, slopped water into them. The horses churned up and down in their loose boxes.

'Get back, you slob,' I said, shouldering the first one, who did a U-turn and went straight for the bucket.

'Nice to think you're still a virgin,' Columbine said over the door. 'But I have a lot to do. So get cracking.'

'And who cleans the horses?' I asked, as water from the other bucket seeped into my sockless sandshoe.

Columbine adjusted the buckle of her belt with one of her public smiles and said: 'You do!'

'Where's Joe?' I said. 'Your so-called fiancé.'

'No need to be sarcastic.'

And before I could answer she was gone.

> Summer time was nearly over,
> Blue Italian sky above.
> I said: 'Lady, I'm a rover,
> Can you spare a sweet word of love?'

I combed out and looped up the previously acervated manes, holding the rubber bands in my teeth.

'Nancy is half Italian,' I reflected, which might account for her getting on so well with Nicholas; the cosmopolitan touch.

> She whispered softly: 'It's best not to linger'
> And then as I kissed her hand I could see.
> She wore a plain golden ring on her finger.
> 'Twas goodbye to the Isle of Capri.

I gave the two horses a cursory rub with the body-brush and by the time I was finished she was back.

Nicely timed!

Joe was with her; he looked chastened as if he'd been recently brought to heel, and as Columbine led out the champion horse, Oloroso, he gave her a leg up.

'I have to go home,' I said, 'and fetch in the black pony.'

'Hang on till I've finished exercising, and we'll have a drink.'

Joe took out Furioso and vaulted on to its back; a fair and organised couple.

Joe's woollen interior was coated in a brand new maroon blazer.

I began playing patience on an upturned crate. Hooves clattered on the cobbles. I cut and shuffled the cards.

'How are the gee-gees?'

The burning question!

That's what they all said to each other, praying for spavined hocks and sprained fetlocks.

And later, when we were installed in the Horse Show Bar:

'How are the gee-gees?'

'I hear Kellets got a new horse!'

'Since when?'

I stood beside Joe, penniless, in the dark.

'Oh ho, the sister,' said a man from Meath with stone blue eyes.

'Sex and the gees. Can't be beat!'

'A smashing filly!'

Joe stretched his arm through the mob and extended two shillings. He wore woollen mittens. I moved aside from the Meath man.

'Where's the horse from?' Columbine asked.

'Couldn't tell ya.'

'Maybe galloped over the border with the white bread!' Ha ha ha ha . . .

> South of the border down Mexico way,
> That's where I fell in love, when stars abov-

'Quit up,' the barman said.

'Give me tenpence,' I said to Columbine. 'I've no bus fare.'

'Give the child her bus fare.'

Columbine was smiling. Her collective smile.

'Columbine!' I hissed.

'What what?'

'I have to catch my bus.'

'Oh yes,' she said. 'And don't forget the blinkers.'


I caught a tram and we sailed down Northumberland Road.

The Ballast Office clock was striking the hour as I raced down to McBirney's and leapt onto the step as the bus slid down the quays.

The slow single-decker bowled along by the park, over the Liffey at Chapelizod, past the Dead Man Murray, through Palmerstown and up the hill to the Hermitage Golf Club. What excuse could I drum up between now and Leixlip?

None.

What excuse can I give for staying out another night?

Nicholas and Nancy are angels of tolerance.

Nicholas and Nancy are . . .

The driver took the steep hill into Lucan at breakneck speed.

The bus stopped outside Sarsfield House.

Teas: 1/-

Leixlip: 1¾ m

Tell him nothing.

Collect the pony and ride back to Dublin.

Nothing.

Say nothing at all.

At Doran's garage the residue of travellers got off.

They knew me; I knew them. We passed in silence.


'Did you bring in the blinkers?'

'Jesus, I forgot.'

'The team hasn't a snowball's chance in hell now,' she said. 'You know Furioso has to have the shades or he'll refuse the first fence. Joe'll have to borrow a pair, now, before the competition tomorrow.'

'I thought I was riding him.'

'Ah, no, childe,' Columbine smiled her special smile, the one reserved for me. 'Joe knows the leps better than you do. You've never been round the big course.'

She began to shovel straw in a businesslike manner. 'Come on,' she said. 'You've got Nizam.'

Napoleon sat on a black horse. Its name was Nizam.

'He's got a gammy knee.'

'Might hold,' she said.

I bedded down the animal, closed the door and sauntered off. I sauntered through the Main Hall, this establishment of wealth and wonder. People were still making last-minute adjustments to their stalls. Gnomic women with tweed faces like their wares.

I preferred the Annexe, where I could collect samples. Nugget boot polish, Kolynos toothpaste, Scott's jams.

Yet I lingered at the stall belonging to the *Irish Times*.

Major J. Flume Dudgeon, with lopsided humorous smile, in half-profile, shook hands for time's eternal eccentricities with the President of Ireland.

Next week, I reflected, Columbine's photograph will be on display. She will be holding a silver cup and shaking hands with the Hon. Mr Justice Wylie.

I turned and 'Talk of the devil,' I said.

'Where do you think you're going?' she said.

'I whispered softly: It's best not to linger, but when I kissed her hand I . . . ' I said.

'Where?' she said.

'To Nicholas and Nancy's.'

'Did you tell the da?'

'No.' I said. 'But I'll phone tonight and tell him I've missed the last bus.'

'I'm going to the Metropole tonight with Joe. You'll have to go home.'

'I've been invited back to Nancy's tonight.'

'You're going there this very minute?'

I started walking towards the exit.

'Wait!'

I increased my pace.

'Wait!'

We were both hurled through the turnstile like rubbish.

Outside she dragged on my sleeve.

'Hang on a minute.'

We were beside the grille that said: Queue Here For Change.

'We'll sort it out,' she said.

'We will?'

'Of course, childe.'

'How?' I said, suspicious.

'I'll get Joe to cadge some petrol. I'll cover up for you. We'll go to Leixlip tonight.'

'Thanks,' I muttered.

'That's settled, so. And now, since I've an hour to spare, I might as well come with you.'

I gazed at the metronomic procession of humanity that passed to and fro.

I gazed at her, huntress, dancer, Artemis . . .

No.

'No,' I said. 'No. You'll find them boring.'

'Oh ho. Well in that case,' she said. 'In that case, I tell you what, let's have one more drink before you go.'

One more drink before I go.

We re-entered the Horse Show Bar.

It was empty.

We sat gloomily in the gloom.

'Two gins and limes,' Columbine said.

The lime is free.

A man came in with a dachshund. He ordered two sherries. The dog put his forepaws on the table and lapped up the drink.

We nudged elbows.

'Good dog tray is happy now, he has no time to say bow-wow,' I said.

The dog curled up on the chair, watching his master with a deep velvet frown.

'Why do you want to see Nicholas? He's ancient isn't he?'

'Not that old.'

'Is he a cousin?'

'Second cousin once removed.'

'Is he the one we pushed into the septic tank?'

'That was his brother.'

'Must be very ugly.'

'Why?'

'Because I remember him now. He was nearly bald.'

'He has receding hair and buck teeth.'

Columbine burst out laughing.

'What does he do?'

'He . . . because he was in England when the war broke out, he was called up. He's in the Intelligence. He's teaching English to Polish refugees so as they can teach English to Polish refugees.'

'So as they can teach English to Polish refugees.'

'Yes, so as they can teach English to . . . '

'And who is this Nancy person?' Columbine yawned.

'Surely you know who Nancy is?'

'Why should I?'

'Because she's married to another cousin. William.'

'Who's he?'

'Oh, he doesn't enter into it. They're separated.'

'What's this we did to him that time?'

'Read his love letters.'

Two Irish army officers came into the pub; she jumped up to join them at the counter.

Commandant X tapped the bar with his silver-topped cane and ordered her a drink.

She slid her smooth hand along the counter and all the little sentences came bubbling out. The two soldierly men, the flowers of the Irish team, alternatively fawned and basked in the presence of my sister, Columbine de Vraie. For a portion of a minute, I sat where I was; then, sliding from my seat, I headed for the door.

'Hang on a minute, childe.'

I stopped.

'The sister!'

'Oh,' said Commandant X.

Commandant X said to Captain Y that severe cases of thrush

were often due to the horses having been left out all winter in bad clover land.

And Columbine said that Westmeath was one of the worst counties for this and both the officers said that this was extraordinarily interesting. I said that I knew a man who had a horse with thrush and he cured it by giving it a bottle of Guinness every day. Both the officers turned to me.

'And yes,' I said. 'It's amazing how they get to like it.'

They both turned away.

'Most quadrupeds,' I said, 'take a liking to alcohol if given half a chance.'

They both looked again, very closely, at me. 'Oh,' one of them said.

Dusk blunted the ugliness of Ballsbridge as we crossed the Dodder, passing the elbow of rich living of Clyde Road, Elgin Road and Herbert Park.

'And do Nicholas and Nancy really know nothing about horses?' Columbine said.

'I don't think so.'

'Sounds utterly haywire,' she said.

We took up a stance at the tram stop in Northumberland Road.

The tram from Dalkey hove into view. It clanged up Merrion Road like a giant on roller skates.

Would she really go?

She did.

She jumped on this city-bound vehicle and, swinging on the vertical bar, shouted: 'Be good. And if you can't be good be . . . '

The *careful* went spinning down Northumberland Road, obscured by the rattle, unheard by me.

On the off chance that Julie de Vraie, Columbine's younger sister, might be able to present to the world a personal identity, individual and untarnished, she proceeded down Lansdowne Road. She sauntered along between heavy mansions on the left and a leaf-lined footpath on the right, where, beyond and alongside it, grew different species of trees and bushes, the evergreens dark, the deciduous pale, but all green, green, green.

Come along for supper!

That's what they'd said to her at breakfast time.

She was heading for that careless invitation from Nancy.

She was heading for Nicholas' trenchant opinion that something could be made of her.

They had lent her their charm.

Nicholas, scholar, aesthete, and handsome as a cat, had a remote disposition, yet he had interrupted his life-long tête-à-tête with Nancy to smile upon the girl.

Julie stopped in the centre of the road. She went on. She stopped again.

They might have forgotten!

She reached the wicket-gate that led to Nancy's house.

She stood there till a light went on in the front room. It was Nancy who had lit the table-lamp.

Julie could see her quite plainly bending over a grandfather chair; she heard Nicholas' voice from within it.

She couldn't see what they were doing after that because Nancy came to the window and drew the curtains.

She heard laughter. Humorous talk. More laughter. She walked to the hall door and knocked.

'It's on the latch.'

She turned the handle and went in.

'There you are, my dear,' Nicholas said.

Julie sat down on the third armchair.

Nancy got up and filled a tumbler with water and whiskey.

'You look in need of this.'

'Did we not enjoy our day?' Nicholas said.

'I had a terrible time,' Julie said, hurried, as she took the drink and smelled it. It was the same as last night: beautiful. 'I groomed the horses . . . '

'Hmm . . . ' Nicholas said.

'Columbine, of course, rides the roan horse, he's the champion . . . she . . . '

'Hmm,' Nicholas said again.

'You're not listening,' Julie said.

'I am a decrepit old man and don't deserve your company. You are delightful. Less about the horses, however, but tell me more.' Nicholas' tones, whether mild or vexed, were very rich.

'I'm sorry. You see Columbine is really the boss. But I know that the habits of horsey people are boring.'

'You are the first person who hasn't bored me for ages,' Nicholas said.

'You don't have to be shy and secretive with us,' Nancy said. 'What are your plans when you leave school?'

'To get away,' Julie whispered, barely audible.

'Do you miss your mother?'

Julie looked up at the far wall. She didn't miss her mother one bit. Her mother had expected her to look people in the eyes. She sniffed her drink with forlorn intensity.

'This is lovely,' she said.

'Whiskey is good for the soul,' Nancy said.

Nicholas looked at Julie, said to Nancy: 'I still think Freud has only half the answers.'

'You never commit yourself.'

'Would you say my thinking is jejune?' Nicholas laughed, manoeuvring his eyelashes and biting his bottom lip.

Nancy, laughing with him, answered: 'I wish I did.'

'I shall be a very old man when I qualify,' Nicholas said. 'If I take my pre-med this autumn, I shall have to return to Cambridge when the war ends.'

'An artistic setting for your middle years,' Nancy said, yawning and stretching her hands along the inside of her knees.

17

'Your dream is an amalgam of unanalysed impressions, my dear. What do you think, pretty coz?'

'I?' Julie said, dumbfounded. 'I . . . I think it's great.'

'Our cousin thinks it great,' Nicholas said.

'She has insight,' Nancy said.


Julie wanted to be quite drunk. She worked her way through the second glass of whiskey as quickly as possible. The badinage, the intellectual rapport between Nicholas and Nancy, filled her with envy. She saw stars and deserts as their talk circumnavigated Nicholas' imminent departure. Nancy said he would be a very old, very discerning psychiatrist one day. Julie sank into mists of anonymous drunkenness, not drunk enough to join in. She gazed at the Roman arch that divided the room in two and beyond at the transparent stillness of the sky framed by the north window. The moon, like a silver coin, was flying through the lacy clouds. It was all at a great distance from her.

'She belongs here, don't you think?' Nicholas said.

Nancy came from a background of Spanish scholars, musicians; her sister was an Oxford don. She packed a cigarette into a long black holder:

'If this damn war was over, she could live here with me.'

'Did you know there was an aqueduct at Leixlip?' Julie said. 'There are otters there. In the winter, if it freezes, stalactites hang from the stone ceiling.'

'And one year,' Julie continued, 'I found a fox. A cub. I tamed him. It was peculiar.'

'She is like a Spartan boy. The Spartan Boy,' Nicholas said. 'Do you think I should marry her?'

Nancy looked, suddenly, like a tired gypsy who has told too many fortunes.

'I think you should,' she said.

'She'll be grown up when I qualify,' Nicholas laughed.

'She could be your Rousseau's Emile.'

'Anyway,' he turned to Julie, 'when I get my next leave, we'll honour that theatre date we didn't have last night.'

Julie said nothing.

Her face, turned inward, was blank with apprehension.

Nicholas said 'Hmm', and turned again to Nancy.

'Should I try to get her a job in England?'

'She could learn typing,' Nancy said.

'I speak fluent French. I got a Latin scholarship last year,' Julie said, bucketing out of her numbness.

'Shall we put her in charge of de Gaulle?' Nicholas slurred his speech under his crooked teeth and smiled like the devil that could hoodwink the fools of the world.


Although they talked about her as if she wasn't there, Julie stayed with them till Nicholas eventually rose as a signal for bed. While Nancy bent to extinguish the lamp, Julie waited expectantly, hoping for a gesture or a touch. But Nicholas stood with his limbs all loose, looking down at her; looking right into her.

He drew a line across her forehead with his finger.

'Don't be too tough,' he said.

Julie ran out of the room and up the stairs to her allotted bedroom and Nicholas called after her: 'You will send me a line, won't you?'

# PART II

# 2

Sawing on the mouth of a heavy chestnut horse, a fiery brute, with a blaze face and four white socks, I caught up with my employer. The latter, an elderly gentleman with a Chaplinesque moustache and steel-rimmed spectacles which matched his spikey hair, gave his head a semi-circular twist at the sound of the approaching hooves.

'Ge-hur,' he said.

'He's beginning to come to heel,' I said, as I thundered against his mare, a calm, well-bred animal, who changed feet at the impact but kept walking.

'By the time your grandsons arrive, he'll have settled down,' I said, as my mount bounced along crabwise.

My employer, whose name was Lord Girvan, allowed a fleeting smile to wander over his pink upper lip: 'I never wanted a girl for this job,' he said.

We rode on in silence, the hooves whispering on the untarred road that bordered his demesne.

It was another sunny day. Ever since my arrival at Girvan Castle, the sun had shone relentlessly; it was worth a comment.

'Should be good for the crops – this weather,' I said, combing a hazel twig through the horse's thick chestnut mane; it snorted and hauled on its bit. Lord Girvan said nothing.

'Of course, I know that a May drought can be damaging to the potatoes. But the farmers complain of everything, don't they?' I continued.

The fifth Earl of Girvan twisted his rigid body and gazed at myself, his new groom; he distrusted the way I sat, with short leathers like a jockey; not rising to the trot, I bumped along nonchalantly, my elbows on my knees, as if I was reading a book.

'Did you ever hear the old saying,' I said, nervously: ' "One white sock, buy him; two white socks, try him; three white socks, look well about him; and four white socks, have nothing to do with him?" '

We reached a field-gate inset in the repetitive blackthorn hedges.

'In here!' Lord Girvan muttered.

My horse shunted impatiently as I bent down to undo the piece of twine that held the gate shut and a flock of sheep darted through a gap in the furthest fence.

'Get that gate seen to,' Lord Girvan said.

'I'll tell Brennen.'

We slid through the aperture and took a few genteel turns around the field at a slow canter. When the lord had had enough, we went back on the road and jogged off in the direction whence we'd come.

Passing through the main gates of Girvan Castle, we trotted up an avenue of chestnut trees, greasy and tough, till the arch of greenery rose into open space. To the right was a large Regency-fronted house, three storeys high, whose windows caught and reflected light from different angles. It had a modish expression on its countenance.

To the left was a paddock that sloped away behind herbaceous borders. Sloped away to infinity, almost – the distance being chopped up by low hedges and scant fields – Girvan Castle had originally been build at the top of a hill to keep the enemy at a disadvantage.

The lord dismounted stiffly. He dismounted cowboy fashion, stepping off, leaving the left foot in the iron until the other was established on terra firma, and then he straightened his military frame. He tugged his grey knitted waistcoat downward and, throwing the reins on the mare's neck with a final 'ge-hur', he strode up the six steps that led to his hall door.

As soon as he was out of sight, I whipped the two horses round and trotted smartly back down the avenue and turned off on to the path that led to the side gate to the yard. The gate was set into the massive wall that surrounded the stabling; I had to dismount to force back the heavy iron bolt.

Once unsaddled in the yard, the animals made a beeline for their individual stables. I groomed them in turn with wisps of straw, finishing off with the chamois leather and a slap. I put the harness in the harness room and went to a double-sided bin and scooped out five measures of oats.

At one o'clock, a huge cloche bell, hanging under a Gothic arch that divided the lower stables from the upper byre, clanged from side to side.

'Not before time!' I came out of one of the stables, stubbing out a forbidden cigarette. The boy hanging out of the bell-rope saluted me.

'Aye,' he said. 'And I'm quitting.'

'You're not!'

'I am that.'

'What's up?'

'Brennen!'

'That creep. But for God's sake don't leave. Every cloud,' I said, 'has a silver lining. Even a perpetual cloud like your man.'

And I left the yard and went into the servants' hall for dinner. That evening, I attempted to write to Nicholas. I attempted to tell him where I was and what I was doing. But the letter written, and re-read many times, made no sense. I tore it up and went to bed.

# 3

'Do the cups!' Nellie said after breakfast, her eyes watering.

'I see a journey, Nellie,' I breathed, shaking the deposit of tea leaves and unstirred sugar beneath a rim of orange lipstick.

'And a tall handsome man in his late sixties.'

'Mary, mother of God, that'd be the lord. Is there anything like the sack in it?'

'Well, I wouldn't exactly say the sack. But there are two crossed knives beside your plate!'

'I knew it,' Nellie said. 'When I left the lady's nightgown on the samovar this morning.'

I was lingering as long as I dared. The lord's movements were predictable; he toured the yard every morning shortly after nine. Nellie, too, was protracting the last few moments of freedom before the scramble of her work began, before commencing her daily shuttlecock existence as servant to the servants, the lowest of the low.

'Don't worry, Nellie!' I squeezed her shoulders as I jumped from my chair. 'We'll survive, you and me.'


I mucked out the stables, swept up the brown urine that channelled between the loose boxes, and stepped out into the sun to await my employer.

Apart from Bella, a Cottage mare, good blood, good bone, the other four horses were of indifferent origin.

Lord Girvan and I rode out every morning, he on the thoroughbred, myself on one of the other beasts, while he sniffed out his acres and amalgamated his thoughts for the coming day.

He was late.

By now, geared to his autocratic ways, I attempted a campaign of invisibility; if he saw me properly, he'd shoot. My Woodbines, rationed to last me the week, were running low. There was a flush lavatory in the yard for the use of the labourers; I went in there for a smoke.

I heard steps. I stubbed out the fag end, stuffed it back into its packet and stepped out with a welcoming smile.

'Ah, Julie! I was just coming to look for you. I was up at the castle and they told me that I'd find you here. How about a spin with me?'

Instead of Lord Girvan, I encountered a small vulpine individual, to whom I'd spoken outside the parish church the previous Sunday. He was the bishop's son, James Poynton.

'Ah, but,' I said. 'I have to take Lord Girvan out for his constitutional.'

'He has a meeting with my father this morning. In fact he's over there now; they're prattling away. I got tired of listening to them and I thought of you and the sky and open spaces.'

'I see,' I said, looking into his small sour face.

A spin with James Poynton?

'When'll he be back?' I said, doubt rising.

'He couldn't possibly return before lunch.'

Oh well, I reflected. 'Would you mind fetching my bike from the shed? I'd better not be seen down there at this hour.'

He looked uncooperative but, nevertheless, went off to get it. After a mile along the tarmac, James swivelled off to the left. He was well ahead.

'Hey,' I shouted. 'Where are we going?'

'To the lake.'

'Which lake?' I yelled.

'The one beyond Ashford. It's actually on my father's land.'

27

Like Lord Girvan's, the episcopal acres stretched over the county.

'I hope we don't meet him. God.'

'He's too lazy to walk that far,' he roared.

'Bishops are never lazy,' I screamed.

James took another turn; this time into a boreen.

I don't fancy you.

Bump.

I don't even like you.

Bump.

Through wild garlic woods we rode, in this nightmare fashion. All right for him on his Raleigh sports.

And there was the lake. One of those plain flat ones, with marshy edges. A heron crouched, his mournful shoulders the epitome of patience. A nervous mallard blasted off the water through the rushes.

'This will do,' he said, laying his Raleigh carefully on the ground.

'I must be a nitwit,' I said.

'Why?' he said, imperious.

'Never mind,' I said, sitting down on the damp moss.

'We haven't much time. Take your knickers off.'

'No.'

'Yes.'

'No.'

There is the smell of milk on your saliva.

'We must practise what we preach.'

'I don't preach anything. I just don't want to.'

'You silly little girl.'

He grabbed my hair. He glued his sharp wet face to mine; his glasses bumped against my cheek. He threw them angrily on to the grass.

He heaved and panted and groaned as he pumped up and down on my rigid body. His trousers were halfway down his legs; the belt ripped my thighs.

'Get off. Get off,' I screamed.

'Keep quiet,' he rasped.

I was terrified. I kneed him in the groin. He fell back. I leapt to my feet.

'You foul bitch. You led me on at church.'

'I did not!'

He was searching myopically for his glasses.

'There they are!' I toed the grass by his nose. He snatched them and, holding the lenses, stamped them on his face. 'You'll answer for this,' he swore.

He'd tell them. He would. Twist the story to his advantage.

'I'm sorry,' I said, to protect myself. 'I really am.'

The heron spread his great grey wings and flapped ponderously into the air.

This was lunacy.

'You see, I haven't, you know. I'm just not like that.'

'I thought you were different. You're so young and healthy. You know the sort of girls my mother has around. Dumpy sweaty bags like the Dean's daughter . . . '

I saw his point.

'If it wasn't for my play . . . I'd go mad . . . mad . . . ' His voice rose soprano.

I picked up my tangled machine and started pushing it up the slope from the lake. He followed me, muttering: 'You must read it.'

'Sorry?'

'My play.'

I was, at that moment, concerned only with returning to Girvan Castle before my absence was noticed.

'Yes, yes,' he kept on. 'It's great. Eugene O'Neill couldn't do better. But my mother will be shocked. She probably'll never talk to me again. These things must be said, you know, Julie.'

'I see.'

'You're not listening.' He was disgruntled.

'Oh, I am. But I must get back.'

Glad of the tarmac, at least, I pushed ahead of him.

'Sorry I misjudged you,' he said, his short legs pistoning beside mine.

You misjudged yourself, as well, I thought, trying to keep in front.

'But I'd like to see you again. When can I?'

'I suppose we'll meet on Sundays. Same place, time,' I said.

'Why do you go to church? You don't believe in anything, do you?'

'I find it very boring. But it's easier to go than not.'

'Ah,' James said, importantly, as though on the brink of a great dialectic discovery. 'Do you believe in vampires?'

'Vampires?' I said, puffing up the last escarpment that led to the back gates of the castle. 'I don't think so.'

'Then you are a heretic.'

'How so?'

'I'll explain when you're older.'

How dare he think he'll know me when I'm older!

I sped past the lichened gate posts. He had dismounted at the entrance but I waved a hand, indicating, I hoped, that our acquaintance would be minimal in future.

The farmhorses were clattering down to the trough and the scaly old man who minded them had not seen his lordship. I went gratefully into the cool harness room and lit a cigarette.

# 4

On the box-lined path that ran from the side-lawn to the stable yard, I came face to face with Lady Girvan. We both stopped like cars on a narrow road until I squeezed into the hedge to let her pass. Neither of us spoke.

I'd eaten my dinner, amid temperament and chaos, in the long baronial servants' hall and was returning to my equestrian chores. In the yard, the horses munched rhythmically behind their red-painted doors. The immaculate cobblestones which I'd swept before dinner trapped the nerveless heat. In the harness room, nothing had been touched.

Logic didn't enter into it when it came to predicting the lord's movements in the afternoon; from time to time he might enter and utter some joyful monosyllable like 'boy' or 'Brennen' which I would have to interpret, but today neither he nor his NCOs were around. Five horses had still to be exercised, so I decided I'd better start. Taking the brood mare and two of the others, I rode out for my first stint.

I turned left at the back gates in the direction of Girvan town.

Lord Girvan's cousin, Emily Cooper, lived along this road. Her house was behind the matted uncultivated wood, and my three horses automatically stopped at her gates. They were open, lying aslant on their hinges, and my cavalcade passed through and jogged up the avenue. The out-reaching branches brushed the lead horses' coats like friendly hands.

Miss Cooper's house was long and low and dropped to a gable end. The upper storey consisted of six dormer windows, overgrown with insistent ivy that proliferated almost to the eaves. The gutter had a sinister sag here and there. The whole gave the impression of a structure fast sinking into the earth.

I shouted out: 'Miss Cooper.'

A swallow left its nest and swooped down over the grass. I called again. I stood in my stirrups to peer into the drawing room, which occupied the left-hand side of the house. It was empty. I rode round the side; the hooves swished through the foliage, a distant corncrake repeated its cacophonic call, and the young rooks chattered in their craggy nests high up on the branches of a beech, but there was no sign of human life. The lead horses pulled on their ropes and tried to graze.

Then she appeared; her arms were full of dead flowers. She hurled the burnt-looking stalks to the ground and said: 'We'll put the horses in the yard, shall we?' And she hurried off, her long legs taking short steps, her narrow body jerking under her silk dress. The backs of her shoes slid off her heels with each step. Her house, her yard, her fields were all part of the estate; Lord Girvan's cattle used her place as a stomping ground and, skirting the muck, Miss Cooper dashed across the yard and opened a door, inside of which was a row of stalls, and into these stalls my charges gratefully went, glad to be away from flies and further exercise.

'What shall we do?' she said.

'Are your new hybrids well?' I asked.

'Sulky but alive. Shall we visit them?'

She was off again.

We entered the house by the back door. Her companion, May, a woman of unparalleled hostility, was blocking the damp scullery; her tall, respectable bicycle leant against the wall.

May was dressed in town clothes — tweed suit, white shirt and neck tie, grey hair ironed out and imprisoned in a net. She did not acknowledge my 'Good afternoon', but Emily only giggled and squeezed past and flew off in the direction of the narrow passage that led past disused rooms, dairies and out-offices, encased in their fungoid smell; a smell that pervaded the entire back portion of her ancient dwelling.

'Hang on, Miss Cooper,' I shouted, blundering behind.

'Call me Emily,' she sang back. 'We're nearly there.'

She was fumbling with a mortice key when I caught up with her; it locked the last panelled door that led into her greenhouses, and we stepped out into a blaze of light.

'A pretty Victorian name, don't you think? Highly unsuitable for a dried-up old stick like me.'

And down she went into the central path, tracing her fingers along the moist soil of the hip-high beds.

'They look healthy.'

Some robust green-yellow shoots had recently pierced the earth.

'Time will tell.'

I read the labels: '*Laelia Purpura*: Peru'; '*Orchidium Microchilium*: Bolivia' . . . Each species with its country of origin was neatly penned in her Victorian hand, and behind the front row of young plants were taller ones. Some had solitary blooms, delicate like porcelain and shiny, and behind again there were fern-like growths that cast pencil shadows.

But Emily, oblivious of everything except her passionate interest when she was loosed among her plants, had escaped into the central part of the house that rose like a mosque to contain a swollen jungle which spumed in the heat.

'This is my favourite.'

She slapped the trunk of a stunted palm.

'I call him Diogenes because he never gets farther than this tub.'

I said I thought it looked more like a one-legged lady with an elastic stocking, and Emily laughed like a robber.

'What would happen if I squeezed one of the cacti?'

'It would probably spit at you. I hate them too. They remind me of dusty old spinsters in furnished rooms. I don't know why I grow them. I suppose because they're so tough.'

She began to expound on temperatures and moisture: 'I had to persuade Gordon to adjust the heating. I discovered I was roasting instead of cosseting some of the plants. It's costing him a fortune.'

I dreaded the claustrophobia that attacked me each time I entered her greenhouse; some occupation was needed to offset it.

I righted a watering can.

'Shall I empty these weeds?' I picked up the wheelbarrow. The child's book *Peter Rabbit* came to mind.

'Where's Mr McGregor to shout: "Stop thief!"'?'

'That's what they'd love to say to me,' Emily said.

'But you do all the work yourself,' I said. 'I don't see what they have to worry about. How do you keep the furnace going in the Emergency?'

'Turf,' Emily laughed. 'You wouldn't believe it, but the ministry issued a whole pile of leaflets early on in the war, as to how to work slow-burning stoves on our native fuel.' She was heading for the door at last. 'And Gordon arranged it all for me. He's very good.'

I thought of my mornings with Gordon, the fifth Earl of Girvan, and I wondered would I ever see his good side.

'He seems shy,' I muttered as we entered the Stygian passages. 'If there's anything I can do? They don't always take me seriously. He comes over about once a month to keep an eye on me.'

I trooped after her shadowy form, feeling as cold as the centre of the earth. But scatty and eccentric, she hummed her little song and we emerged into brightness and summer, normality, and May still stuck at the sink.

She took me upstairs: 'To give me something.'

It was pleasant under the eaves; warm and dry. A central corridor with rooms on either side; the floor sloped. I wanted to run.

She opened every door; rattled away like a museum guide. In one room there was nothing but the carcass of a blackbird. She picked it up by its stiff yellow legs and hurled it out of the window. I wouldn't have done it; I was afraid of birds, dead or alive.

'This is my room,' she said with a humorous bow. 'It's in a shocking state.'

Trivia pared away at the bare necessities; white. White walls, bedcover, jug, basin and solitary picture, in which snow predominated. The room was untidy. Heaps of books and catalogues were strewn on the floor. There were clothes on the bed, shoes here and there as if they walked by themselves. Stubs of candles and stalagmites of wax. Liberation in chaos.

I wanted to kneel on the floor and read the titles of the books but I didn't get time; she was off again down the corridor.

'I always tell myself I'll clean it tomorrow. And tomorrow. And this,' she said with her hand on a door handle, 'is her ladyship's apartment. I think we'll leave it to the vagaries of time.'

'Do you think she keeps a cobra?' I said.

'Now now,' Emily said, and her face rippled into gleeful laughter.

The rest of the rooms were like the basement of an antique shop.

'The Anglo-Irish aristocracy did a lot to extend Queen Victoria's Empire in the old days,' Emily said. 'Mostly junk. Is there anything you'd like?'

She was right. Elephant table, carved buddhas. Indian screens, pearl-inlaid escritoires.

'I shoved it all in here and leant against the door,' she said, in the same equivocal tone. 'This is nice.' She picked up a light ebony cane which had an ivory handle. 'It might come in useful.'

I took it and twirled it like a music-hall entertainer. I didn't want it but I thanked her and we both felt embarrassed.


'There you are, Miss Emily.' May, entrenched in her permanent oasis of displeasure, scowled at both of us.

Emily whistled through her teeth with assumed indifference but her mouth became a shade thin as she went off to wash her hands; I followed May into the drawing room.

'She's been up to her tricks again?' May asked.

'She seems in great form.'

'That dashing around's a sure sign.'

'Sign of what?'

'She'd be off, and there's no catching her.'

'Where would she go, in the name of God? Would she take a train?'

'The sooner you stop encouraging her, the better.'

'But she's lovely.'

'Lovely to you. You don't have to mind her when no one's around. When you come in she's all "ha ha" and "how's your father".'

I burst into uncontrollable giggles. 'What's she ever done that's so terrible?'

'You don't know.'

'Does she go out on moonlit nights and howl to the moon?'

May looked up at the ceiling for astral intercession.

'You're very ignorant. And bad-mannered. I had to fetch her in once. Dripping wet.'

'Did she fall into the lake?'

'Stayed out in the rain all night.'

I stopped laughing. I looked beyond May, beyond the small Sheraton desk which contained Emily's notes, beyond the window and the tall yellowing grass and all the sunny centres between trees and shrubs, and I saw a tall woman walking. In the dark. In the rain.

She came in. She came in sideways, her eyes lowered, avoiding May's, and sat stiffly down. We ate in silence.

When May went out for a moment, I said: 'I hope I'm not rocking the boat.'

'You're keeping me alive.'

'I take up a lot of your time.'

'You must continue to do so.'

There was no time to talk. Her companion – a companion who was, in reality, a mental nurse, was back to fuss and scold, and all the old Protestant horror rose up inside me. Don't touch, don't kiss, don't, don't, don't . . . God's watching . . . God's in your pocket . . . God's in your knickers . . .

'Emily,' I said. 'Don't think me rude . . . I've more horses to exercise before six . . . '

Mundane chatter like butterfly kisses round a candle.

God. Oh God!

I touched her hand. Pumice stone. I ran the knuckles of my fingers down the edge of her cheek. She looked up quickly, as I'd once seen my mother look up at my father after a similar caress.

She said, 'You'll come tomorrow?'

'Of course. Bye bye. Cheerio, May.'


The following afternoon she was standing on tiptoe outside her hall door, clipping back a grumpy-looking rambling rose. *Claque claque* went the secateurs; I could hear it as we paddled up the avenue.

'There you are.' She waved the secateurs in an arc. 'I told May to lie down.'

I wanted to mock May but said nothing and, knowing this, Emily said: 'We mustn't be uncharitable,' with the lips impish. 'Come along. Can you stand the greenhouse for a minute?'

'Of course. I'll just put the nags away.'

*Claque claque.* A summer sound. Quite normal.

'You'd never guess,' she said, 'but I've had a letter. From the Cambridge Botanical Society. They want me to unravel some point about subsoil. Apparently there's been a hell of a row, which resulted in the resignation of some big cheese.'

She was off round the house, full speed, as usual.

'They were fighting about *Orchidia Microtis* . . . my pet subject.'

'You must have a universal reputation,' I yelled as she diminished in the greenhouse.

'Not really. I once published a very unlearned paper and let the cat out of the bag.'

'Quite a cat.'

'I don't know. I'm so rusty. Now if I was in Brazil or Peru still, I'd have something to say. But I'm just a dotty old woman pottering amongst her plants.'

She bent down and gathered minutiae of weeds.

I felt unaccountable joy at the thought of Emily's telling some Cambridge scholars where to get off. This was justice.

'You'll write back?'

'I spent the morning poring over my book. But these ancient pedagogues don't really interest me. Of course I'll write back. As politely as possible. If only I were in Chile.'

'All those South American countries,' I said. 'You must know the place like the back of your hand. How long were you there?'

'About four years.'

She turned her back and began to weed where no weeds were.

'Which were the nicest parts?'

'Chile,' she whispered. 'Went to Valparaiso to meet a friend and she didn't turn up.'

'Valparaiso!' I rolled the word round my tongue.

'I went into the desert. Yes.' Her voice was staccato. 'I had a great piece of luck. Yes. My passion for grubbing around for strange growths. I had an introduction.'

She got up and walked down the length of the glasshouse.

'I met this guide. He was as interested as I was. We didn't have jeeps in those days. Lucky to get a mule to wear away your heels. Such a fascinating terrain. You've no idea . . . '

'Oh Emily, you've no idea how I envy you.'

'Unfortunately it all ended like a Victorian tear-jerker. They kept tracing my movements. Through the local consul and so on. Very tiresome. Then they heard. Two young people in the desert. And I wasn't that bad-looking when I was young.'

Taller than I, her small head was turned towards the inner door. The girl. The old woman. Young and beautiful. Damn it; still elegant, personable, pretty; stuck in this godawful place.

'Could you not have stayed?'

'An uncle came out post haste. I suppose at this distance it sounds comic. To save me from this "dago" . . . '

She put her hand to her forehead as if she was trying to pierce the spindrift of time.

'Are you all right?'

'Yes, yes.'

She took a few short steps and suddenly stopped to sit on the low wall. Her hands hung down, making a well in her skirt, the old cotton gloves a mass of wrinkles.

'It fitted together so nicely for them. It was found out that he was bespoke to the daughter of a neighbouring ranch. He was quite rich.' She gave an ironic chuckle. 'They found out everything.'

'Oh Emily, if only . . . '

'So many "if only"'s . . . '

'Yes, but was there nothing?'

'When he arrived . . . my uncle . . . I ran out into the desert alone. I wanted to be what I *was* . . . myself to them – mysterious, perhaps ignorant. But it didn't work. I didn't go far enough.' She got up. 'It's all in the past. I am being dramatic.'

She ran towards the exit and I followed her.

'I'd made my mother ill with worry. Inexcusably selfish. Yes, I realised this when I came home. Oh well. Lah de dah, such is life. Come along.'

When we came into the scullery, May was there. Emily said, sharp: 'Miss de Vraie is hungry,' as though it was an old story that never quite ends and is always interrupted by this phrase.


That evening I roamed the roads on my iron bicycle.

The gaps in the hedges flashed past. Dark and light. Light and dark. Blackthorn, blackthorn and more blackthorn. Beasts lumbered in the fields. The corncrake rapped out its message. *Crr crr.* Like an unanswered telephone. Over and down the small humps in the road went my bike, dithering in the potholes, sliding on the camber. The country closed in with its lumpy hills, scanty farms, small squares of fields awful with poverty, lean, stony, uncultivated.

I cycled on into Girvan. The main street snaked away on either side: cluttered like an eighteenth-century engraving, shopfronts leaning. Bar and groceries. Groceries and bar. 'O'Hanlon's Victuallers for prime meats'. Only the Majestic Hotel, with its four pillars and portico, extended into the street like a hopeful merchant. Halfway down was Mooney's Hardware.

Having drinks with Mooney had been one of my diversions when I had come to Girvan a few weeks back, but the astonishing energy of Brennen, Lord Girvan's leg man, herd, agent, and what have you, who made it his business to know mine, so unnerved me that I hadn't been in lately.

The hardware shop was shuttered. I shoved my front wheel against the door and banged with my knuckles. I called up: 'Des.' Before sending me packing on the Girvan bus, my sister Columbine, with dovelike sympathy, had given me Des Mooney's name; a bastion against the aristocracy. But now not even Des Mooney was around.

Several times I shouted, but no one came. I cycled down Main Street. I heard a familiar voice: 'Such a nuisance.' James Poynton's unmistakable drawl. He was accompanied by a figure in a mustard-coloured frock around which a cotton jacket was tightly buttoned.

'They do like a laugh, once a year, poor things.'

This must be Mrs Howard, the chemist's wife, organiser and begetter of the Girvan Dramatic Society.

I watched them clopping along.

'We'll have to scrap the act altogether,' she bayed at James, 'unless we can find a stand-in.'

I longed, insanely, to call out: 'Let me do it! I'll dance and sing and entertain!' but they were gone down a side street. They were gone, conspirators in the heavy summer night, rich in anticipation of their creativity.

# 5

'Are you off?' Nellie said.

'I am not,' I answered. 'I'm damned if I'll go to church this morning.'

'What'll their lord and ladyship say?' Nellie said, wildly clinging to a load of linen.

'It's all right for you. You've been to Mass. You should hear the clergyman: *Naou to Gawd the Father, Gawd the Son and Gawd the Holy Ghost.* And that after an hour of hell and damnation from the pulpit.'

'Lord save us,' Nellie crossed herself.

'But honestly, they put the fear of God in me. It's not fair.' Yet it was easier to go than not.

Hovering in the doorway of the little church on its wind-drawn hill I was hailed loudly by James. His family – the bishop and his wife and daughter and retinue had sped down the hill in their open Citroën and were piling out like partisans come to free an occupied village – and Lord and Lady Girvan, and various members of the quality, brown, brown, brown, some with counte-nances like bark and others with faces polished white and with heavy jaws, were milling around me.

Lady Girvan nodded and Lord Girvan said: 'Let's get on,' and into this theatre of the absurd filed myself and the rest of the community.

Every Sunday the hunchback dressmaker attacked the keys of the harmonium as if they were scalding her and the deep bass voices of the women and the contralto of the men blasted into Gothic infinity. My stomach growled through the thunder of arthritic kneeling and rising while Lord Girvan changed his spectacles before he read the lesson, and through hymns and psalms, until, at last, everyone was loosed among the *tick-tock* of the insects in the grassy churchyard full of *joie de vivre* and condescension.

After dinner I walked along the Girvan road. I climbed on to a field gate and, taking a Penguin book from my pocket, began to read. A woman, wheeling a high pram, and a thin girl with quick eyes strolled past me. I guiltily hid my book, unable to challenge them with even the most modest remark about the weather. I climbed down and idled off in the direction of Emily's.

'I shouldn't think you'll be welcome!'

'Is Miss Cooper out?'

'Miss Emily's having tea with his lordship,' May said, sneering emphatically.

'Oh, in that case . . . '

I glimpsed her as I retreated down the steps; gay as a geisha girl; she was twirling round as she waited on her cousin.


The following day Lord Girvan rode ahead as usual with long stirrup and straight back; he gave his head a half-turn, like John Wayne.

'Hope that horse will be ready for my grandsons.'

My horse bounded forward into its bit, kicking great clods of earth into Lord Girvan's chest.

'It will,' I said, and we bounced along side by side.

A mile farther on, he said: 'You see a lot of my cousin, Miss Cooper.'

My stomach contracted and my knees tightened round the pommel of the saddle. But he said no more. He said nothing; did not even answer my query as to when his grandchildren were due to arrive. When I delivered him to his hall door, he simply stalked up his front steps, his lips very pink under the dark moustache.

'When are the children due?' I asked Nellie at lunch.

'Next week.'

'My God. So soon!'

'Mind your language, Miss de Vraie,' said Tom the butler.

Fuck you, I thought.


That afternoon the sun danced like frost on the cobbles.

Running about, cleaning the harness one minute, grooming the horses the next, I humped saddle and bridle on one of the horses and, taking the other two, mounted in the yard in the usual tangled mess. When I looked up, there was pigeon-toed James; he'd come in and left the yard gate swinging.

'Shut the gate,' I said crossly.

'Why, Julie,' he said, 'not your usual laughing self.'

'Mind,' I said, hoping the horses would stand on his feet.

'I've good news. My play! It's finished! And it's great! I want to celebrate with you. I'll take you to all the nightspots in Girvan.' Full of fun, he was.

'I can't come.'

'Why not?'

'I'm busy.'

'I, too, have to think up excuses. My mother doesn't approve of you.'

I gazed down at his face. The occasional hair sprouted from the little pockets of acne on his chin. Sunshine was cruel to this strained individual. I gathered my animals in line and made to depart.

'Come on, Julie, let bygones be bygones. I'll call round for you on my bike.'

I decided, 'Why not?', and told him I'd be at the Majestic at eight.

'Could you not make it earlier?' he said, never satisfied.

'No,' I said, exaltedly stubborn. 'See you in Girvan.' And I trotted out of the yard.

As I drummed along the tarmac, I could think of nothing except the stabbing economic efficiency of Lord Girvan when it came to causing me pain. Even my visits to Emily had to be made in secret from now on; moving around in any way other than five paces behind him constituted insubordination. I raved internally as my cavalcade beat up the dust: I won't listen to him – I don't care what he says; I'll visit Emily whenever I feel like it, today and tomorrow and the day after that, and all the days I'm in Girvan I'll continue to visit Emily. And this very night I'll call on Des Mooney and drink with Des Mooney, member of the lower classes, criminal and hardware merchant, and all the people in and out and around Girvan can say and do what they bloody well like. And if James Poynton thinks I'm under an obligation to him to do anything I don't want to do, I'll bring all my powers of imagination and energy into the fray and he'll regret the day he ever was born.

In a state of frenzy, I rode past Emily's gates, and a mile or so farther on I turned the horses and rode, in a state of frenzy, back. I'll kiss the wind and throw flowers through the impenetrable trees, and if they strengthen their ramparts with moats and estate walls and *chevaux de frise* I'll still find a way of getting through, like wind along a telephone wire, because love is tell-tale and stupid but it's also determined.


'Des!'

The hardware shop was in darkness, but at least the door was open. 'Are you out in the back?'

'Julie.' He emerged from behind a pile of wire netting. 'Thanks be to Jees you're here.'

He picked me up and swung me high on the counter. 'How's my fashion-cover girlie? My little mascot. I haven't seen you for ages.'

'I came looking for you Saturday night.'

'I was over the border.'

'I guessed.'

'Dunwoody, the Customs officer, has gone for his tea.'

'Will he talk?'

'Fuckin' eejit. Still, there's nothing they can pin on me. Nah, Uncle Des is too clever by half.'

'What is it this time?'

'Same old thing. Bicycle tubes, wheels, spares, but it can all be shipped to Dublin at the drop of a hat. Never mind. Let's have a jar.'

And he shut up shop as I leapt from the high counter and we entered the bar of O'Hanlon, brother of the butcher and second to none when it came to pulling pints.

When Des' stout and my small brandy were reposing restfully on the table, Des said: 'What's happened you? You were in every other night when you came first, and now I hardly ever see you.'

'They're all watching me. Brennen, for instance, the herd. Slings up the window every morning and reports on my movements. And I do eff all.'

'Orange bastard. Don't mind him. He's nothing else to do.'

'And the lord! The less said . . . Even Miss Cooper's sort of out of bounds . . . '

'Never mind, childe.'

'But I can't stay shut in there for ever. Like the princess in the tower.'

'Miss Cooper doesn't exactly run a den of vice. A decent stick. I once took her cow to bull and she gave me tea in the drawing room. No side. But May!'

'Do you think she's mad, Miss Cooper?'

'Nah. It's convenient for them to say she is.'

I looked into my crystal drink. How I loved it. I held it high till the last drops ran into my mouth.

'I know she's not,' I said.

I hadn't yet gathered the courage to tell Des I was going to meet James Poynton. We'd had several drinks, and the thick air of

O'Hanlon's sealed us off from the thin atmosphere of the outside world.

But I had to tell him.

'Des!'

'Yes.'

'I'm sorry, but I have to go soon.'

'That's all right, childe, two more large ones and a monster ginger ale.'

The barman, who looked twelve and was probably fifteen, whipped away the empty glasses and replaced them in a few seconds.

'Going for the big time,' Des said.

'You're drinking brandy?' I asked.

'Never mind me. Why do you have to go?'

'I have to meet James Poynton, the writer. At the Majestic.'

'I beg your pardon.'

'What I mean is, he's leaving his mammy and taking to pornography as a full-time substitute for the umbilical.'

'Eh?'

'I don't mean that at all. Don't take any notice of me. He's just a slob, but I'm going to clean out the episcopal funds. He wants to buy me drinks! Imagine!'

'We'll have another before you go,' Des said, short.

'Don't withdraw. I'm not gone yet. And besides, this is a secret between us, because if you would, would you spring me later? I'd hate to spend the night with him.'

Des looked intensely lonely suddenly and I felt tremors of fear. Refusing to give favours to James might be easy enough, but Des, his shiny suit clouded with grease stains, his heavy mournful hands and his large face, was another thing altogether; I stumbled as I rose, knocking the bench.

'Please,' I said.

'OK. But Julie.'

'What?'

'You're getting drunk.'

The sun was still lying over the house when I went into the street. Clipping along on my high-heel shoes, I could feel the lace curtains being fondled behind the low windows. A man was leaning his elbow on the straddle of his donkey; the cart rattled when the animal moved. He looked nonchalantly at me, with the representation of a smile on his lips. I nearly smiled back.

With head down, I ran towards the Majestic and burst into the hotel as if my clothes were on fire.

James Poynton sat back in his armchair, reading the *Evening Mail*.

'Hello.' I subsided into the chair beside him.

'There you are,' he said, his eyes swivelling to the clock.

'It doesn't matter,' he said, like a sick grannie. 'Do you need a drink?'

'Need?' I said. 'Yes. A brandy.'

He winced.

'A brandy and a bottle of er, ahem, do you have a good brand of beer?'

Already slightly drunk, I focused on the barman, a mere boy too.

'Getting younger every day!' I said, bursting into uncomplicated giggles.

But I tried to pull myself together, to anticipate an enjoyable evening. James looked so uncomfortable in these surroundings of rep and linoleum; his pointed, uncooperative face did little to enhance the atmosphere. I decided it was do or die.

'Have a Cairns!' I yelped.

'Well boy,' James said. 'A Cairns!'

The barman, or boy, tongue-tied in face of this anomaly, hastened to the shelves.

'Oh,' I said. 'I've made a momentous decision.'

'Eh?'

'Yes yes,' I rattled on. 'I've decided not to go to church any more.'

James looked in the direction of the bar and sipped his drink as if it was medicine.

'I'll drink it if you really hate it. As a chaser.' And I moved the coaster in my direction. 'And you have a pale dry sherry. Do you have sherry in the palace?'

I felt wads of painful laughter in my stomach. Not much of the fairy prince about James.

'My mother is rather keen on her cellar.'

'Cellar? Do you have a cellar? Full of old hock and stuff like that? I must visit you sometime.'

Seeing his expression, I said: 'Don't worry, I was only joking.' Dense!

'Anyway, did you hear me?'

'You said you weren't going to church any more.'

He sipped his new drink, which was clearly more in his line.

'I think you're wise. Unfortunately I have to pay lip service to my father's oratory. But then I am a Christian.'

'You are?' This was a new slant on things.

'And obviously you're not!'

'I see.'

There was a silence. I wished I was in the kitchen with Nellie, looking into the tea leaves.

'That your play in there?' I pointed to a briefcase I'd just noticed at his feet.

'You must read it. But for God's sake don't lose any of the pages.'

'When I was at home, my aunt took me to see *Ghosts*.'

'What did you think of it?'

'It was marvellous. Sybil Thorndike was in it.'

'Ibsen is the great god of the theatre.'

'I thought you said it was Eugene O'Neill.'

'He's good. But beside Ibsen he's a journalist. But I'm dying to know what you'll think of my play.'

Was he?

'Did you do any acting at school? They say it's best to learn the trade the hard way. I did. I used to play all the kings in Shakespeare. Well some of them, anyway. But I got more kicks out of acting and producing a play I wrote myself.'

'Oh,' James said, with difficulty.

'Oh yes. It was called *The Alarm Clock*. The clock, you see, has a terrible time. And its owners. It ends up going off in a symphony concert. A girl called Joyce O'Regan took the lead. She was one of the owners. The other one was a dreadful girl with black teeth. Miscast.'

James interrupted me by laying his hand on my knee.

'You're a natural.'

'A natural what?'

'A natural is . . . '

'No no, don't tell me. It's someone who doesn't know what they're doing.'

I subtly moved my knee, and his pale hand dropped with a bump. 'That could sum it up,' he said, rather huffily. 'You see, Julie, when you're as old as I am, you'll know the score. When you've read all the books I've read, you'll know what has to be said. Sex, for instance.'

I recoiled.

'No, Julie, sex is part of life. Not something apart from it.' He spoke with a nasty squint, like a marriage-guidance counsellor.

'And is that in all the books?' I asked, deliberately ingenuous.

'Have you ever read anything?'

I had read all the books in Foyles' twopenny lending library in Leixlip. It was a positive fount of literature. Secretly and solemnly I'd worked along the shelves.

'Have you ever heard of Edgar Wallace? Or Sidney Horler? Or Ethel M. Dell?' My voice was rising. 'Or a great black book called *A Century of Mystery and Horror*? And *Tales of the Imagination* by Edgar Allan Poe? Or *Crime and Punishment* by Dostoevsky, or *The Winding Trail* by Zane Grey? I'm telling you,' I said.

He said Dostoevsky was the single cherry in the cake, and I asked him what his play was about.

'It will astound the critics. They are, unfortunately, the ciphers of public opinion. A necessary evil.'

'Are they?'

'Can't you ever be serious?'

Oh fuck, I thought.

'The plot?'

'It's about love.'

'Ah.' A relief.

'A young boy from a public school falls in love with a woman twice his age. But his sister, who's in love with him, can't bear it. She interferes.'

'Sounds like Electra.'

'I thought you said you'd only read trash.'

'I said nothing.'

'Well anyway . . . ' he continued.

'Don't tell me the ending.'

'The ending is conventional. She just shoots herself with a gun.'

'What's she doing with a gun?'

'Don't be a fool, Julie. Don't you know anything about poetic licence?'

'No. But I know a hell of a lot about gun licences and how hard they are to come by.'

My flippancy infuriated him. So what! We weren't in church.

Nor in the wild garlic! Ugh!

'So there is a dramatic ending. Which one, actually, shoots herself?'

'The sister, of course.'

'How very sad.'

'Life is sad, Julie.'

'Are you telling me?' I began to laugh.

'What are you laughing at?'

'The spirits have improved my spirits. Ha ha ha.'

50

James twisted with embarrassment. I changed the subject. 'I went to tea with Miss Cooper on Saturday.'

'That old nut!'

'God!' I said.

I snatched my empty glass and sucked in the remnants of my drink.

'She isn't a nut!' I was really angry.

'Oh come on, Julie. I thought you knew the score.' That score again.

'What score?' I shouted. 'She's saner than anyone else around. She's more intelligent than the rest of them put together.' I wanted to say 'You' but didn't have the nerve. 'She's been hammered down by the iron of intolerance.'

'Really, Julie. You're a child.'

'I am not. And if you call me a child again, I'll . . . I'll . . . '

'Behave yourself. You really ought not to see so much of her. Lord Girvan would be very displeased.'

'You're dead right, and you're talking like him now.'

'I know. But, Julie, you'll only unsettle her.'

'Fat lot you care.'

James got up from his seat.

'Wait!' I said, pounding my fists on the arms of the chair. 'She had a letter from the Cambridge Botanical Society and — '

'You believe that?' James cut in. And then he gave a loud guffaw. 'And you saw it?'

'What do you mean?'

'You've had one over the eight!'

I laughed maniacally.

'Of course I haven't. And I didn't. I mean what I mean is I didn't want to see the letter. I know it was true. She knows everything there is to know about South American plants.'

'The stupid old plants are there. She has to potter about doing something. But you mustn't believe what she says. Why do you think May is there? Do you know what she is?'

'A disgusting creature. That's what she is.'

'Really, Julie, you are silly. May is a state-registered nurse.'

'I don't care if she's the Queen of Sheba. And I know people say Emily's mad. The servants laugh at me for going to see her. But I know differently. You'll tell me she was never in Chile, I suppose.'

'Oh, she did go there, I believe. But it wasn't till she came home that she started to behave so oddly.'

'Wouldn't you behave oddly if you'd been caged in like a lion for the last fifteen years?'

'You're getting hysterical over nothing.'

'Nothing!' I screamed, getting up with the intention of yelling for more drink. Then I suddenly saw Des.

'Des!'

James spat out: 'Do you know this person?'

'Des,' I screamed again, waddling towards him like a prostitute.

'Come on, childe,' Des said. 'I'll see her home.' And staring through James, he took my hand and dragged me from the hotel. The last glimpse I had of James was of a creature full of incomprehensive horror at the sight of this member of the lower orders.

Drunken tears splashed down my cheeks. 'It was the letter!' I kept raving.

'I don't care whether it's true or not. If he thinks he can make me think like them, he never will. Never never never.'

'Shh, childe.' Des hurried me along Main Street and into the nearest bar. 'I'll settle you down and get a hackney to drive you home.'

I wouldn't settle down. I ranted for more drink. It was as if my soul was oozing away from my body and only the drink could save me.

'*The Case of Mr Valdemar*,' I yelled. 'They kept him alive till black liquid oozed through the ceiling from his room.' I laughed hysterically.

I didn't budge till I was paralysed with alcohol.

I'd been crazy enough to entertain the notion that James and I might be friends, and I pestered Des with questions till the barman refused to serve me and I was dumped in the taxi. I heaved and vomited in the back seat, and when I was finally unloaded at the yard gate of the castle I lay against the gatepost, retching, till my stomach could retch no more. I was dimly conscious of a light on in the byre, and then Brennen, of all people, stood over me, holding a storm lantern.

I ran. Doubled up with cramps, hoping in my befuddled state that he didn't realise I was drunk; I ran and I didn't stop till I'd reached my room and immediately passed out on my bed.

# 6

'Quick, quick, it's late. The bell has gone.'

I was in a deep, deep sleep. Every aching bone and muscle screamed for more rest.

'I ca . . . n't . . . get . . . up.'

'Are you sick?'

'Sick, Nellie, sick. Oh God.' I groaned.

'Can I get you anything?'

'No, Nellie, you go. You'll get into trouble. And thank you for waking me.'

On the floor, I fell straight on my face. I lifted my spinning head to a vertical state and then dragged my legs after the rest of my body, diving for the basin of water. I put my whole head into the basin and scraped my hair to get rid of the smell. I picked off little crusts of vomit with my nails, like removing nits. I'm in a fine shape to meet a new day, I thought, as I staggered out of the room, tripping over my high-heeled shoes, which seemed to be scattered all over the floor.

I was still drunk.

The stairs were steeper than usual, the corridors more gloomy, the distance between my room and the servants' hall peopled with phantoms of a more obscure and twisted nature than usual. While I gulped my scalding tea, the window shot up. There he was, as always: Brennen, in collarless shirt, serge trousers riding up his chest, braces, one button inevitably missing.

'Had a lot on board last night.'

Every servant stopped chewing. Six pairs of hostile eyes turned on me. The one ally, Nellie, tried, but failed, to intervene.

'Oh, my head.'

He mimed a sick head by holding his hands over his eyes. The first titters of laughter went round the table. They grew into massive peals.

'Split your sides, it would.'

'Good morning, Lord Girvan.'

'Miss de Vraie.'

'The sky is grey,' I said nervously.

He looked at it and sniffed.

'Date's fixed for the fifth!'

My stomach heaved. I rushed into Bella's stable and tea came down my nose. I tried to sniff it back and nearly died. I snatched the chamois and wiped my face.

The date! The sack!

'Race,' Lord Girvan said.

'Good idea,' I said, trying to look into his inexplicable mind. I pictured Lord Girvan and myself haring across the front lawn. Weight and age in my favour, I should pull away nicely and reach the tape a good ten lengths in front.

'Congratulations, Mees de Vraie.'

I could see Lady Girvan's smile like a vision of security.

'You may have your initials carved on the cup and the date.'

But of course the old sphinx was talking about the gymkhana held every year on the front law of Girvan Castle.

Annual charity. District nurse.

'Yes, Lord Girvan. Bells should win. Will we have bookies?'

'No, I don't think we'll have bookies.'

'Tell the young fellow to start lopping that old Scotch fir below the pond. Then the two of you can fix the jumps in the afternoons. If you come to my study at twelve, we'll map out the course together.'

I harnessed Bella and one of the other horses, whom I had christened, with some originality, the Beast.

'Do you know what day it is?' he asked.

'Tuesday.'

'And what do we do on Tuesdays?'

'Visit the tenants.'

There were twenty-five hands working for Lord Girvan. His estates bordered the county. He had at least a thousand acres of woods and so-called arable. The small lumpy hills and scrub-filled valleys made the going hard but these men kept Lord and Lady Girvan in tea and sugar and return tickets to the House of Lords, which is somewhere in London. On Mondays, however, Lord Girvan checked over his cloven-hooved population, hunting the fractious creatures into corners, dividing ewes from wethers, sniffing with satisfaction at the numbers of fat marketable lambs; the last of the Irish cowboys. And on Tuesdays he rode from tenant to tenant, wearing his bland abstract smile, as each in turn bade him the time of day.

'We'll start with the Brennens.'

Mrs Brennen, come to the door and cringe before the lord and master.

'How are the children?'

'Very well, thanks be to God, and thank you, milord.'

'The peas?'

'The rooks is something terrible this year.'

'Fierce!' I interpolated.

They both glared at me as if I'd farted.

'Chicken's laying?'

Mrs Brennen puts on a conspiratorial air and looks in my direction.

'Lord Girvan, Lord Girvan. Did you see it? The fox? There he goes.'

I stand up in my stirrups. 'Lord Girvan.'

'Do you think it's not getting on?' I timidly asked.

'Yuss yuss. Whuff whuff.'

She'll get another chance next week, I thought.

'Tell your husband I'll expect him at the Lodge tonight.'

'Aye, I'll remind him. Terrible forgetful he is these days.'

Not half-forgetful enough!

'Goodbye, Mrs Brennen.'

'Remember me to her ladyship.'

Hard to forget you, Mrs Brennen.

# 7

Lunch is ready.

Lord Girvan mapped out the gymkhana course.

He expounded on his ideas for a set of jumps as if he was reorganising the cosmos.

His servant, Julie de Vraie, stood silently by. She neither acquiesced nor disagreed with his plans but behaved as a servant should: ductile, obedient.

'You will start at four. The lad will be sent down to help you then.'

'Lunch is ready, milord.' Tom knocked for the third time.

'All right. All right.'


'You often visit Miss Cooper?'

So saith the lord!

And the bishop's son saith: 'You'll only unsettle her!'

And God sits up in his cloud, smoking cigarettes, and he saith nothing whatsoever.


I took my three horses down the Girvan road and wheeled up her avenue.

There were pencil grooves of uncertainty on her forehead; her lips were in a straight line: 'I was so afraid you'd stay away.'

She ran ahead of my cavalcade; her silly shoes, slopping off her feet, had to be retrieved every few steps. As she bent down, all her bones protruded and her tussore dress shone like steel.

'You should have come in on Sunday . . . My cousin . . . '

'It doesn't matter.'

We sat on the grass among the rhododendrons till I made a bed in it, flattening it out, staring at the cotton clouds trafficking in the sky. She sat upright beside me, and from my angle the clothes-peg pinches of time that ran from her chin into her neck looked like streaks of mud. With her solid little head cocked, she said: 'I often wonder why you ever came to Girvan.'

When I didn't answer – for there was no answer – she said, hurriedly: 'It has the worst of both worlds, the Protestant and Catholic. The bigotry is frightening. Sometimes I wake up in the middle of the night wondering how it will all end. One day there's going to be a terrible reckoning.'

'Most people don't care; they're either too subdued or too complacent, it strikes me.'

She laughed cynically: 'I have a lot of time to think. Before you arrived, I'd spend weeks on my own – except for May – and well! I'm a bit uncouth, you know.'

'I don't think you are.'

'When I got back from South America, I made a botch of everything. I didn't do any of the things expected of a country spinster. I didn't play bridge or tennis or follow the hounds or open fêtes. Instead, I used to ramble off for hours at a time, refusing to speak to any of my family. My mother was delicate and, as you'd say, she took to the bed. My father stormed around till she died and then he had a stroke. I suppose, in his way, he missed her. It was surprising, because he was very strong. A gloomy, determined man. So it was a case of nursing him. He lived for about four months afterwards. He was paralysed. I was haunted by his silence, wondering what he was thinking about, wondering if he, too, saw his life as a botch. One gives them credit for nothing until it's too late.'

I felt gloom descend. I gave my own parents credit for nothing. Did not intend to, either. But Emily was in the middle of the end of her life and she saw things from the other end of the tunnel.

'You make me feel as if I should go home and look after my father,' I said, trying to make light of things, but Emily was sharp about this and said if I went back, I'd be there forever.

'Needless to say, I've thought of that. My father and I . . . '

'You've never met?' Emily said, her girl's smile brightening her face at last.

I told her then about Nicholas, and how I longed to leave the country, as if the country was to blame for everything. And she laughed and said how she'd felt that when she was young, and said how the war had sliced up our lives now and nothing would ever be the same again.

'People like you and me,' she said, 'have to trap our experiences when we're very young. I was lucky. There was no war to prohibit me. But you must think me very chicken-livered to have given in to them in the end; to have limped home with my tail between my legs?'

'In your socks, I'd probably have done the same.' Emily hugged her bony knees.

'To all appearances, I was a demented young woman. They meant well when they employed May to look after me. Yes. They were honestly concerned about me.'

'They were?'

Lah de dah, as she'd said. Such is life.

Was there a flame to be rekindled, I wondered? Would she up and go again, given half a chance?

The young lad was waiting for me at the fallen fir.

'Sorry I kept you.'

We dragged a branch out of a clutch of undergrowth. I thought of tea and peace.

'This is murder,' he said, wiping his brown face with a rag.

The cross-cut pinged as it caught in the notches.

'Let's tear down the telephone poles,' I said, and he hunched his shoulders and giggled through his nose.

'What about the bushman?'

'Saw the lady in half.'

The windows of Girvan Castle stared at us with their centuries of complacency.

'It would be great if a German bomber came and flattened out the house. What do you think they'd save first?'

'Save themselves, most like,' he said.

We sat down and smoked and I waited for the iron to enter his soul. Before he reaches forty, I reflected, there'll be an accumulation of iron. We went on working.

We sweated and cursed and accomplished nothing. The earth breathed its pungent breath, innocent of our attack, which left no mark. When the great yard bell clanged six, we gratefully laid down our weapons.

'Tomorrow and tomorrow.'

'Aye,' he said.

'Will we chance leaving the cross-cut out here for the night?'

But Girvan Castle shrugged its shoulders and I picked up the thin blade and let the handles dangle at either end: ping pong.

'Cheerio, miss!'


'Got the jumps up?' Tom asked at tea.

'Just like Ballsbridge.' I glared at him.

'A lick of paint now . . . ' Tom, the leader of the claque, looked round the table to gather the titters from the other servants.

'All right,' I said. 'You should try the useless bushman . . . '

'Useless bushman . . . ho ha he he he . . . '

Ho ho ho!

I sat alone in the servants' hall long after the tea was cleared.

'What's up?' Nellie said, back and forth with her endless carryings. 'You're fed up. I'll get you some cake.'

'Tell me about the younger generation,' I said. 'Are they any better than the old.'

'The lord's daughter; she's a humdinger all right.'

'The honourable Mrs Travers?' I said, doubtfully.

'That's her!'

'Any other good news?'

'The kids are pretty.'

'All kids are pretty,' I said gloomily.

'And what happened to her husband? Did he get killed in the war?'

'He got a cold in Canada.'

'It's a cold place. Did he run away?'

Nellie's laughter broke like a thunderclap.

'I'd die if it wasn't for you, Nellie. And Miss Cooper.'

There were purple wells round Nellie's eyes as though someone had punched her.

'You slave from dawn to dusk and no one gives you credit for anything.'

We parted at the fork of the back stairs. Nellie went off to her small cell and I went off to mine.

My room was cluttered with cheap furniture. One window looked out on the lawn that rolled south. The architects must have built the house at night; the front of the house trapped mere splinters of the morning sun and the rest of the day it remained in shade. But under this side window Lady Girvan reclined each afternoon in her deckchair and occasionally her husband joined her with his straw hat tilted down to his square moustache. The other window looked out on the back yard; noisy work-worn cobbles echoed the clatter on the days when the herd's wife, Mrs Brennen, came to do the churning or the laundry. Laundry days were gale days. Steam came out of the sheds as though Stevenson's rocket was parked inside; water raced into the shores, and the servants raced out carrying linen and baskets of underwear.

At the heel of the yard, the grumpy remains of the original castle, a mottled heap, was used for storing corn. The original Girvan, an English earl, must have had little to do except hurl the odd lead ball on the natives. Not much change, I reflected, as I drifted into sleep.

# 8

'Mare ready?' asked the fifth Earl of Girvan a couple of afternoons later.

What do you think she's doing, standing there harnessed to the trap?

I silently stood while my employer fumbled with the door handle of the bockety vehicle.

'Can I help you?'

'Whuff!'

He finally yanked open the door and I simultaneously leapt into the well of the trap and, imagining myself to be Boadicea, we plunged down the avenue.

'Steady, girl!'

We skedaddled on to the tarmac. The lord was silent; a proud man!

The mare settled into a fast trot and I was imagining that, with any luck, while the lord does his business in the town I would be able to get Mooney to buy me a drink, when he started stammering orders . . .

'In here . . . [sniff], will you. Brace of pheasants . . . my cousin . . . '

We wheeled into Miss Cooper's drive, the vehicle keeling at a dangerous angle and the whiplash leaves snapped at our faces. 'Here we are,' I said definitively, thinking I'd never better do that again or I'd not last another week.

I was afraid to look at Lord Girvan. Afraid to see the old man, with his underlip hanging, his black moustache trembling. But not afraid to be glad if I saw it; to be glad if the whole structure of the Anglo-Irish way of life, with the landlord class and its false mores, arrogance, self-deception, crumbled away in its senescence.

But no. Nothing like this was evident. The lord rose, self-satisfied, if stiff, and, disdaining my offer of help, dismounted from the trap and strode towards Emily's hall door.

We are invisible elements of servility; and you'll get no quarter from me!

I addressed his back, silently, as he lifted the ancient knocker to hammer the worn wood.

Wouldn't you be upset, if you knew I still visited Emily? I laughed and chewed a piece of grass.

He hammered again.

Christ! She'll think it's the bailiffs!

He chucked and clucked and clicked his heels and then hung out of the bell rope.

The tumbledown outhouses stretched to the right, window-high with the grounds. On the left the angular beech tree threatened the gable end.

I plucked a low branch and stuck it into the bridle of the mare to ward off the flies. I chewed a new piece of grass and sat down on a stone.

May, who believed in the relentless pursuit of health, must have persuaded Emily to go for a stroll.

My employer, however, in his lordly manner, was taking their absence as a personal affront. He continued his interminable mutterings:

'Wretched woman!'

I removed the branch from the browband and prepared to mount the trap. Then suddenly there was May! She had rushed out, flinging open the door. Her face flopped over to one side as she choked and heaved. The lord sprang back, saying: 'Well? What is it? A turn?'

'Oh no, sir. Come quick, milord, sir!'

Unable to touch her, he sort of poked her out of the way and strode past her into the hall.

I ran to the steps: 'May. Wait. Please. Tell me. Tell me what's happened.'

'She's done herself in. A rope.'

Emily? Emily Cooper. 'Damn,' I shouted. 'Damn, damn, damn.'

I had nothing to do. I stared and stared at the silent house; the ivy leaned out of the windows. The hall was in shadow behind the half-open door. A breath of wind came from nowhere and ivy rat-tat-tatted as if it was in a hurry, till the breeze, as suddenly, dropped.

Emily!

The pony stamped its feet and swished its tail, distracted with the flies.

What are they doing inside?

Are they hating each other enough to deal unemotionally with one who was so warm and vital and is now cold and gone away somewhere? Nowhere?

The insects ticked and hummed, tearing about, industrious and frantic as if only their efforts could keep the jaded plant going. And there in the deep cool dark house was Emily, all fair and pale and still.

There was the sound of a car. It stopped on the road. I heard the gears change and the slow rumble of the engine as it approached the house. It drove up to the steps and a dapper little man, carrying a bag, jumped out and, running round the bonnet, took the steps two at a time. He, too, disappeared into the house and once again silence. And, like this, more and more people might arrive, and all might run up the steps and be swallowed up in the lifeless building, and they would be efficient, they would be purposeful, and they would change nothing.

'I'll go home with the doctor, Miss de Vraie.'

I mounted the trap and the mare reacted by moving forward.

'Whoa!'

The trap jolted down the avenue. I made the impatient animal walk, pulling in to let the Morris overtake me.

In the kitchen, the servants were all huddled round the Aga. They gave me a mug of tea.

I wandered upstairs and lay on my bed.

I noticed that the ceiling was crowded with small brown cracks.

I gazed at the crazy map till the light went. And long afterward, the map remained in my mind.

The ceiling is cracked!

# 9

I had seen them arrive, the 'county'!

Summer coats and linen hats, with artificial grapes. Decanters and clatter. Silver coffee pots and silver trays, shined like mirrors. His Grace in gaiters; Her Grace-ess in a pale blue coat and skirt, swinging behind him as jaunty as a sailor on leave.

'So nice. So nice of you to come.'

Lady Girvan, herself, as sleek as a tigress, conducting three or four conversations at once. Lord G., his suit blue-black, the trousers knife-edge, his face adjusted to eternal youth, surveyed the gathering with a grave smile.

In the back pew of the church, I sweated it out. Knelt with the others. Rose with the others. Mouthed the hymns, the psalms. Sat for the Pauline lesson. Knelt again for the prayers for the bereaved and wondered who they were. Then the middle-aged clergyman, perched on the pulpit like an owl, had climbed rheumatically down and joined his bishop, who held the mitre like the devil's pitchfork.

Take your knickers off!

His son, James, his face spearing the distance, sat by his mother in the front pew across the aisle from the Girvans, and his mother's fierce soprano rose to the beams.

> Lead kindly light
> Amid the encircling gloom
> Lead thou me on . . .

I had gathered no flowers for Emily's coffin.

I thought of heaven in a sky as blue as baby ribbons. I thought of hell like the inside of the Aga cooker, and I watched the slow crocodile following the wooden box. Six men carried it as though it was a great weight, and she was so light, her head was so small. And then each pew emptied slowly, the front man leading, and the rest in turn, falling into place.

The little graveyard, adjacent to the church, was soon filled up with people. The few working-class Protestants, pushed to the fore, the gentry, with their adjustable grief, stood in exactly the correct positions dictated by their relationship with the deceased. Intensely ill, I waited on the periphery of the cemetery, my hand on my bike, ready to depart.

There was thick scutch grass between the old mossy gravestones but Emily's body was not to lie with these long-dead; there was a neat corner scraped away and they placed the coffin beside a recently closed grave on which was a jam jar of dead flowers.

Emily was struggling with a mule on the foothills of the Andes; she was talking gaily in Spanish to another, who also rode a mule. They took a turn over a sanded hill; the unshod hooves made no sound. There were giant cacti, structured to sit solid in sandy fissures. And the sand rippled and roared and the harsh wind rolled down the hills.

The coffin was laid across the rectangular aperture on a stretcher, and vulgar expensive wreaths fell hoop-la on the upturned clay. As the clergyman cast his handful of 'dust', clinging Girvan mud thumped on the lid of the coffin.

I wheeled my bike out of the churchyard and pedalled hard till I got back to Girvan Castle.


Nellie munched home-made bread. Her big mouth opened and shut as little bubbles of jam stuck to her lips. She licked in the jam and washed it down with tea.

The servants' hall was full of cheer. Tom was ready to burst into song.

Nellie stopped chewing. I put my arms round her. A single tear ran down her nose and splashed on the back of her hand.

'Don't,' I said, stroking the tangled hair from her ears.

'She shouldn't have done it.'

'I don't think she could have gone on.'

The others stopped chewing, telling jokes; they were ready for a bit of drama.

There was nothing in my mind then, except the desire to comfort Nellie. Nellie the slut, dependable, dispensable, like the cheap delft.

But the others got angry. They began piling up plates. They were enjoying the party and this was unseemly. Tom was dying to say something that would cut the floor from under us. He finally blew up: 'That's enough, Miss de Vraie. She's acting silly.'

I placed my cup and saucer on my plate and rose from the table.

'Good night, Nellie,' I said.


For a long time I sat by my window.

The rectangle of grass beneath turned slowly darker in the bluish light. The moon, on the wane, was behind heavy clouds; it emerged for a few seconds and the line of poplars sent shadows shivering towards the pull of the stable wall.

I fumbled for matches to light my candle and tripped over something which cracked. It was the black cane Emily had given me.

'Gordon gave me this for my thirty-fourth birthday, the birth of my spinsterhood. I'd like to give it to you. Not as a symbol; that's a bit played out! But when you get married you can use it to beat your husband!' And when I heard again her thief-like laugh, I felt a darkening of the soul.

I picked it up, tried to straighten it, still unable to find a match.

In the distance there were voices. Quick, like stage whisperings; they came nearer, until directly under my window I heard

Lord Girvan say: 'You are begging the question. She was seen quite late going into his shop. He is very common. It is unsuitable and unpleasant for us.'

'I thought she was quite a nice little thing,' Lady Girvan intoned.

'It is our duty in the war effort.' He continued to pace. 'You must speak to her.'

'Emily was fond of her.'

'Emily!' Lord Girvan snorted. 'Emily wasn't all there.'

Lady Girvan put on her socio-musico voice: 'Very well, I'll do it. If you insist, my dear.'

And the ebony cane is cracked.

# PART III

# 10

During the next few days, Lord Girvan, in a perpetual rage, barked out orders to all and sundry.

He yelled at me for not having finished the jumps, and I ran around half-demented, my fingers torn from hammering and sawing, trying to placate him, with no success.

If Emily's death was offered as an excuse for the slowing down of work, he swore like a soldier.

One morning he was out extra early, and when I reached the yard he was rallying his forces. There was Brennen, mighty and mean, and various other members of his army, and they were crowding round him as if he was planning a blockade.

'And Miss de Vraie!'

'Yes, Lord Girvan.'

'Er . . . my daughter, Mrs Travers, is coming tomorrow.'

As if I didn't know!

'And my granddaughter, Jennifer, needs a leading rein. Is there one?'

'Yes, Lord Girvan,' I said, as I forked the dung.

'Good, good.'

I went out of the stable to get the wheelbarrow.

'And Miss de Vraie?'

'Yes, Lord Girvan.'

'O'Hagan – er, the man we had last year – will be coming to stay for a few days. Mrs Travers will probably like him to ride Bella in the open jumping at the gymkhana.'

I put down the barrow. I felt my lips moving but could get out no speech. I picked up the barrow and wheeled it quickly into the stable, shutting the door with my back. I could feel my whole face queer and stiff.

And the talking in the yard went on.

'Get that Jersey cow down.'

'Of course, milord, I'll have her down directly. And close up Miss Cooper's outhouses.'

Lord Girvan said with repugnance: 'Lucky to get all that over with before the children arrived.'

And huddled, knee-high in the clean, dry straw, I leaned against the mare. I hooked my fingers over its withers and hung there while tears flowed like blood from a wound and made little streams down the pony's hide. The animal sneezed humorously and shook its head, and I still swung on its mane until another 'Miss de Vraie' was barked out and I had to wipe my swollen face with the tail of my shirt.

'If the jumps aren't finished today, we'll have to see what we can do.'

The iron gate squealed as it swung on its hinges.

'Get that gate oiled,' Brennen shouted.

At lunch, I was called to the dining room.

'His lordship would like a word with you.'

I went down the corridor from the servants' hall and through the passages, carpeted and heavily ornamented, where smug nineteenth-century landscapes festooned the walls; I was told to wait in the hall.

The antlered heads gazed hopelessly from their heart-shaped wooden frames and I stood beneath them, waiting for the word within that would bid me enter.

And finally a testy 'Come in, come in' pulled me out of my stupor.

I entered the bright room, which was blazing with flowers and perfumed with expensive meals, and fidgeted.

'Don't fidget. Lady Girvan and I have decided that you're to go over to McClean's yard and have the rest of the timber cut to lengths.'

My mind darted back into a cul-de-sac: 'If your chainsaw had been working . . . '

'You know we can't get parts in the Emergency,' the lord said, as if I'd suggested shooting at the British.

I said: 'Sorry. Where is McClean's?'

'Tom will explain,' Lord Girvan said, and he plunged back into his chocolate mousse.

I ran to the servants' hall in search of Nellie, in desperate need of a friendly face, but when I reached the kitchen, Mrs O'Hagan, the cook, was reading the *Independent*, her spectacles down her nose and the paper aslant the window.

'Where's Nellie?' I tried to restrain my voice from hysterically rising.

'Gone for a lie-down.'

'Nellie taking a rest in the afternoon!'

'She's not well.'

'Today? Or in general?'

'She has a lump.'

'Where?' I shouted.

Mrs O'Hagan folded the newspaper over and halved it. 'In the I . . . soff . . . the throat . . . '

'Nellie?'

Nellie can't be sick because she's never angry. Her eyes fill with moisture that isn't tears. When she wipes her cheeks, it leaves a smudge. When she rolls up her sleeves, her muscles swell and purple veins rise up on the back of her wrists and hands.

'She'll probably be all right with a bit of rest.'


Rest!

That evening I raced into the bicycle shed, extracted my machine and, jumping on to it as though it was the last train to freedom, I pedalled into Girvan town. I strained my utmost in the teeth of the wind.

'Des!' I screamed.

He put his head out of the top window.

'Hold on. I'll be down.'

In O'Hanlon's, we shoved up against the counter; the pub owner was polishing tumblers and placing them along the shelf, shaking out his glass-cloth intermittently as if it was full of crumbs.

'You look rough,' Des said, hamming a half-note on the bar. 'Better have a Jameson. Like a chaser?'

'A Cairns,' I said, swivelling to the door every time someone came in.

'They won't come in here,' Des said.

'It's reflex action.'

'You're cut up about the old woman?'

'God. I keep seeing her. How she must have looked.'

Des put his hand over mine. 'How was she the last time you spoke to her?'

'Fine. Up and down.'

'You were very upset that night about some letter. I couldn't make head nor tail of it. Could that have had something to do with it?'

'No, no. That cheered her up. It was James that annoyed me. The way he jeered at her. None of them took her seriously. Gave her credit for nothing.'

The phrase kept coming up.

'That's what she said, I've just remembered. Dear God. Yes, she said one often gives them credit for nothing until it's too late. Jesus Christ almighty. Des, it's too fucking awful. And I was no use. They hated me for going to see her. But really I was no use ... If I had been, she wouldn't have ... I only went to see her for the sympathy she showed me. Christ, I'm so fucking mean.'

'Stop,' Des said.

The barman had a face like thunder on him.

'Sorry,' I said. 'But if only I'd stopped to think instead of hithering and thithering all the time, I could have done a lot more.'

'Childe,' Des said, his gaze warm, 'there's nothing you could have done.'

He kneaded my back with his fist. 'Would you like a meal at the Majestic? Warm you up?'

'No, no. It's nice here. I'd rather be here. Anyway, I'm not hungry.'

'Same,' Des said curtly, and the barman served the drinks, looking disapprovingly at me.

'Think of the future; she lived her life. Everyone has to go some time.'

'Not like that,' I moaned.

'Whichever way,' Des said. 'And that's one of the quickest. Supposing she had a long illness and no one there only that nurse. How much worse would that have been?'

And after a silence, I said: 'Thanks. Sorry to be so drippy.'

'Don't say sorry to me. How's it above otherwise?'

'The kids come any minute. Nellie seems to be sick.' I started into my drink. 'And Lord Girvan says that man O'Hagan will be staying. Wants him to ride the thoroughbred mare in the gymkhana. And damn it . . . that's the only reason I'm in this ghastly hole.'

'They bloody well can't do that.'

'They can do what they bloody well like,' I said. 'I'm only the fucking groom.'

'Language,' the barman said.

'Sorry.'

Des had endless patience, seeing it was his pub. For years he had drunk here, and he would drink here for years to come, long after I'd left the county. If I kept on like this, he'd be the laughing stock of Girvan.

'I'll calm down.' I began to laugh.

'That's better. For a moment, I thought I'd have to get out the windscreen wipers.' He slapped another half-note on the bar, pocketing the change as if it was rubbish.

He told me the wayward Dunwoody was cooling his heels in jail and we drank to Des' long and successful smuggling career. When we left and night was folding in, we trailed along Main Street, and outside his shop he said: 'I'll get you a new torch battery; that one wouldn't see a hen to its roost.'

He was unduly long inside but I stayed on the street.

'Are you still there?' he called. Then he came out and, with shaking hand, pulled my old acid-encrusted lamp apart. 'Go easy on that curse-o'-God machine,' he said, as he snapped it together again. 'And don't leave it so long before you're in to see me.'

And then out of the town, under the railway bridge and along the ribbon road, and never a sinner to be seen, the old bike bucking in the ruts and the new torch casting an arc of light a few feet beyond the rim of my wheel, till, for one second, it swept over a low hill and illuminated the two sandstone gateposts and the old decrepit gate aslant and buried in the groove of earth. I sped past, as I must, from now on.

# 11

Rest!

'They've arrived!'

You'd think it was the end of the war.

Out in the yard, I waited for the onslaught.

The first to come was the Hon. Mrs Hermione Travers.

'How do you do! Mind if I call you Julie?'

I gazed, with admiration, at this bronze-haired, handsome female.

'I'd be delighted,' I said. 'Come and see the horses.'

'Everything working out all right?' she drawled, as she viewed each horse in turn.

'Here's Bella.' I opened the stable door.

The mare lowered her back nervously at the sight of the stranger.

'She's all right,' I said. 'Always a little fidgety at first, but she'll soon get to know you.'

'Don't you remember me, beauty?' Mrs Travers said.

I stroked the muzzle of the animal, who, reassured, snuggled up against me.

'My father told you, I think, that O'Hagan will be over before the gymkhana.'

I stroked and stroked the muzzle of the mare.

'The other animals, of course, don't have her breeding.'

'Fine bone and aristocratic blood.'

Mrs Travers swirled her dirndl skirt.

The intricate Paisley design made kaleidoscopic patterns in the dust rays.

'Mrs Travers!' I lifted my head and rested my chin on the horse's mane.

'Will you be riding out today?'

'Oh. I'd have to change first. I think the children are tired. A frightful journey. We were hours and hours at Holyhead. Perhaps I'll leave it till tomorrow.'

*Clop clop*, Mrs Travers left the stable and walked out of the yard, across the cobbles in her London shoes, dressed casually for the country. Walking, hips swinging casually for the country.

I stroked and stroked the animal's mane, ran my fingers up its ears and curled round the star that was like a whirlpool on its forehead.

When the gate squeaked shut, I harnessed her and, mounting in the stable, rode out and set off in the direction of McLean's.

About a mile out on the Girvan road, I turned left and, in a fast loping trot, we covered the ground until, rounding a corner, I at once recognised what must be the saw mills; there was a giant haggard, piled high with timber, with its corrugated roof dipping over the road. I went through the gate and called out: 'Hello there!'

No sign of life, so I set off up a track, lined on either side with yew and in the distance a rhododendron, a few desultory trees, one of which was a mangy monkey puzzle – all hinted at some kind of residence.

When I reached it, it was an unresponsive building and looked as though its owner had left in a hurry. I knocked, and the knocker made a dull sound like wood on cloth. The driveway, so-called, was ankle-high in dandelion and a two-tone Ford 8, which had also seen better days, was parked in the middle of it.

I lifted the knocker high and thumped again. No one came.

I wandered round the side of the house, after tying the mare to a stump.

The side of the house was a field. Once upon a time it had been a lawn, but now coarse grass grew right up to the edge of the building, as though in a hurry to demolish it – although an open glass door indicated that it was still inhabited. And right enough, way down in the field was a deckchair, grass to the canvas, on which a figure was reclining while it read the *Irish Times*. There was an open bottle of stout beside the chair, and a bull terrier lying full-stretch on the grass.

The dog leapt up and barked; the figure swivelled round, saying 'About time,' and, seeing a stranger, also jumped to its feet.

'Are you Mr McClean?' I said.

'No.'

'Oh,' I said, backing away. 'I've come to the wrong place. I thought . . . '

'Hold on,' the man said. 'Maybe I can help you.'

'Yes,' I said, halting. 'I'm looking for someone to saw some timber and I noticed the barn, so I concluded . . . '

'I've taken over his business.' The man seemed on the point of deep laughter. 'He bailed out a few weeks ago. Didn't they tell you?' He was leading me towards the house. 'We'll sort things out.'

I followed him through the glass door into a kitchen. It was stone-flagged, and empty, save for a deal dresser and an obsolete coal range, on which stood a Primus stove. A couple of chairs and an upturned butter box made up the rest of the furnishings.

'Excuse this hovel,' he said. 'Will you drink stout out of a cup?'

'Out of a spoon if necessary.'

'Splendid. A girl after my own heart.'

'And I thought you were only Gerry,' he said, laughing basso profundo.

Feeling strangely at ease with this happy-go-lucky man, I said: 'You don't look like Girvan!'

'And Girvan I am not! And never will be!'

There was a poster pinned to the kitchen door; it was the picture of an elongated face and a stretched neck.

'Do you like it?' he said, his eyes following my gaze.

'I think it's lovely. It reminds me of how one looks in a spoon.'

'Intelligent as well.' He expanded his diaphragm and looked searchingly at me.

'I ripped it off a railing outside an art gallery in Paris. That was before this cursed conflagration confined me to my native soil.'

'That's how I feel!'

'But you must be still at school. You look very . . . small.'

'You were going to say "young".'

'There's nothing wrong with being young. Sit,' he said, handing me the cup of stout.

I sat. 'Yes,' I said. 'You can cut some wood for me, then?'

'Where are you from?'

'The castle.'

'An aristocratic sibling.'

'I'm working there.'

'And your name?'

'Julie de Vraie.'

'That's not a name. "Of the true". Of the true what?'

'They pronounce it "Devrey". The "what" got lost down the centuries.'

'And you want some sticks.'

'Planks. Yes. I have the measurements.'

'Well, now, if Gerry were here . . . But Gerry's not here. And where the hell *is* Gerry? Did you see a sweet-natured-looking young boy down at the gate?'

'No. Is he your son or nephew or something?'

He burst out into a deep growl of a laugh. 'Good heavens no. He's my help. I advertised in the *Irish Times* for an intelligent lad, and that was what I got.'

'Why, isn't he intelligent?'

'He's extremely intelligent. But meanwhile I've got to spend the rest of the evening in this dank barracks on my own-y-o. I know. You can stay to supper.'

'I've just had tea!'

'How bourgeois.'

'Sorry,' I said.

'And sorry, too. I didn't mean to be rude. If you wouldn't mind fetching in the stores from the car, I'll start lighting this antique.'

I collected the parcels and he, ripping open one, placed it on the box.

He poured paraffin into the tray of the Primus.

'Worth a mint in Greenwich Village.'

'That's in New York!'

'That's in New York!'

He pumped the machine and flame caught the burner with an even roar.

'A miracle,' he said, straightening up and reaching down a frying pan, on which he placed back rashers.

'Give one more call,' he said, 'in case he's playing Tarzan in the forest.'

I went out and yelled: 'Gerry!'

A squirrel darted up an oak tree, squatted for a moment and then leapt ten feet to another branch. I ran to the base of the trunk but the little animal was camouflaged amongst the leaves.

I went in.

'No sign!' I said. 'I saw a squirrel.'

'They're very beautiful,' he said, almost humbly.


I asked him his name. He said 'Bernard', was mysterious about it, wouldn't tell me his surname. He rocked with laughter when I told him I was a groom, as if I'd told him I was a lion tamer; he said he was terrified of horses. I asked him should his boy, Gerry, come to the castle with a chainsaw or what, and he said he'd inherited enough timber from McClean to build a ranch.

It was arranged that I should come early, 'before Don Juan goes off on his afternoon prowl', the following day.

He came all the way down to the gate with me, saying 'Do you really ride that prehistoric monster?', his uneven features breaking up in merriment, with grape-green eyes swivelling over me as if measuring me up inch by inch. I mounted and rode off, turning to wave, and was surprised to see he looked quite grave. And puzzled.

I cantered along the grass verge, happy as a child on a rocking horse. When I passed Emily's avenue, I involuntarily shouted her name; I was mortified. I searched embarrassedly in all directions to be sure no one had heard me. But there was no one to hear me. I cantered on quickly, hoping against hope that I wouldn't have to see any of the newcomers again that evening.

# 12

'I haven't seen much of you lately. Mrs O'Hagan said you weren't well. What's the matter?'

'It's all right, miss,' Nellie said.

'You need more rest.'

Rest!

Not only had Mrs Travers brought her two sons and daughter with her, there was her personal maid, the little girl's nurse, and a general girl for the two boys.

The English accents of the shy newcomers caused the Irish servants to froth at the mouth, not knowing whether to laugh or jeer. Everyone stared as if at a deaf-and-dumb tea party.

'Let me know if there's anything I can do,' I said.

'You have your hands full.'

'At least I'm finished at six. You have to drag on all evening. For God's sake, take it as easy as possible. I'll do the saucepans tonight for you.'

In the yard I met the children.

The boys' tones were similar to their mother's. They were as shy as I was. They drawled loosely when I addressed them.

Nearly as old as me, yet centuries apart, I felt helplessly unable to probe the dark English veneer of the nobility.

They all rode out, including the old cowboy; the little girl was the epitome of misery, huddled up on the withers of the grey pony, looking as if she was heading for the scaffold.

The Hon. Mrs Hermione Travers sadly disappoints me, I reflected, as I watched the bunch disappear; they all wore dark riding habits and velvet caps and looked like a school of mounted porpoises from where I stood.

The two-tone Ford was parked, as yesterday, in its rakish manner, and when I knocked the dog barked.

A young man came bounding out.

'The young lady from the Castle?'

'Yes.'

'Miss Whadyermacallit from the Castle,' he yelled upstairs.

'Hang on. Tell her to wait.'

Then the figure descending said 'Julie from the castle', and there was a funny smile puckering the cheeks as he said it.

'Shake hands with the lady,' he said. 'And this is Gerry.'

The latter grinned and extended a packet of Players.

'Here's my measurements,' I said, showing him a piece of paper. Gerry laughed at the obvious joke and Bernard said: 'Now, now.'

We all filed down the avenue to the gate, and Bernard said, screwing up his eyes: 'Feet or inches?'

'Feet, of course,' and Bernard said: 'Horses on the ground are bad enough, but flying through the air . . . !'

And Gerry sang, while looking at me:

> She flies through the air with
> The greatest of ease,
> The daring young girl on
> The flying trapeze.
> Her movements were graceful
> All men she could please
> And my love she stole away

And Bernard said: 'Do you hear him?'

'That beastly thing,' Bernard said, when we reached the barn, where I'd tethered the pony and trap. 'I have an aunt who hunts.

She's a class of lesbian, really, and she bought a pony from a couple of what she called smoking children.'

'That was us. Me and my sister. I delivered the pony.'

'She has a *bijou res* on the Dublin Mountains.'

'Yes, I admired the tweed on the lavatory walls.'

'See what I mean! It's a small world. And your name is?'

'Julie.'

'Oh, I remember that,' he said, peering down the opening of my shirt. '*Nom de famille*?'

'Devrey. Spelled "de Vraie",' I said, patiently.

'Oh yes. We've been through that before. "Of the true". Like "Jack of all trades". Huguenot stock.'

'Mixed. My forebears were burghers. An aunt of mine is mad about tracing lineage. She found a pin-merchant on Arran Quay.'

'My lousy forebears come from the North. I wish to draw a veil,' Bernard said.

> King Billie slew,
> The papish crew
> At the Battle of Boyne Water . . .

Gerry sang.

'Get on with your sawing,' Bernard said, in his deep guttural voice, and I burst into laughter.

'You're worse than he is.'

'That's what Tom says.'

'And where do you keep him? Tucked up in bed.'

'Good heavens, he's my sworn enemy. The butler. He makes pleasant little gibes every time we meet.'

Bernard and I sat on a broken wall and Gerry picked up lengths of timber and ran them through the circular saw. Bernard said: 'Stop looking at the young lady's legs or you'll cut your hand off.'

Gerry finished the job much too quickly for my liking. I'd have preferred to sit on that wall forever. But Bernard had time to expand a little.

He unravelled some of the mystery of how he came to be in this county of unqualified hostility. He told me how ever since the war began, he'd had his eye on 'the main chance'. Taking advantage of one war shortage after another, he'd begun by running a fishing boat in Mayo but had had to abandon it, partly because of his profits being shared out with his 'blinding and farting' men. Nevertheless, he'd accumulated enough cash to start a furniture factory. 'You'd like some of the Swedish designs,' he said, and 'I'd rather be nearer Dublin but the bare bones are here. Next week I'm getting some machinery; someone in Offaly is packing in their factory.'

'Why didn't you go and live there?' I said.

'There was no house. Besides, perhaps these hungry little hills suit my personality better . . . They provide strange surprises.'

He took a piece of my hair and curled it round his fingers.

'I see why you like horses. You're related to them.'

A shiver spiralled right through me.

'That's not fair,' I muttered.

'What is?' He sighed deeply with mock despair. 'Tea?' He got up abruptly. 'Things have come to a pretty pass.'

I followed him unsurely into the house. Gerry was humping the timber into the trap; he didn't share Bernard's terror of the animal.

They cursed and argued over the Primus.

'Tell Lord Girvan he owes me £1.17.6.'

'Chreist.'

'What's Chreist about it? He's getting terms because of the charm of his messenger.'

'I was supposed to get the whole lot assembled by the sweat of my brow and the help of a blunt saw and one of his labourers.'

'How much does the old bollocks pay his slaves?'

'About thirty bob a week.'

'Mean varmint' and 'Anyway, give him the bill with my love, and tell him if he doesn't pay, he can stuff it up his . . . '

He swung back in his chair.

'I don't know what I pay you for,' he said to Gerry. 'This place is like a hayloft.'

' 'Tis the cracks that do be in the floor,' Gerry mocked.

'I'll crack you,' Bernard said.

Gerry went out to tidy up the remains of the wood.

'Did you hear him?' Bernard said, his lively features breaking up. 'You'd make a fine couple.'

'I'm shy of young boys,' I said, in a sudden state of anxiety.

'So am I. But in the meantime I have to make do. Unless of course . . . '

'I'm sorry . . . ' I said.

'It's I who should be sorry,' he said. He got off his chair, strangely sympathetic. 'But don't go yet. I'll show you my designs.'

'Are they upstairs?'

We both laughed.

'That's better. You're a bag of nerves. Being with you is like being with a herring catch.'

'Sorry,' I said. 'I always seem to be apologising. I've got the habit. My employers think I'm bad news. And one of the farm workers – Brennen – watches my every move and reports. And the thing is . . . don't laugh . . . I'm as pure as the driven snow.'

'What a boring way of going about things.' He began to look bored.

'Sorry. I'm boring you.'

'No. But I think you must be imagining it. Paranoia. You're doing a very dangerous job.'

At this, I burst out laughing.

'I have to confess that I have no fear of horses. But I'm terrified of them!'

'Who are they, anyway? They're tiny little people.'

'But there's always a "they", isn't there?'

'Poor lamb. Christ, what a place. What lousy sods. The people down South think they're priest-ridden, but up here they're worse.'

I thought of Emily and how she put it.

91

'Yes. Three times worse. Because here you've got a thin stratum of poor Protestants with their craw-thumping, their orangery; it dovetails so nicely into the rich Anglo-Irish landowner's book. And what have they got to show for it? Spinsters, grey-green pimply youths, hot from the dormitories of British public schools. All jolly good sorts.'

'And jolly good shots,' I said. 'You should see the hall of Girvan Castle.'

'How did you get yourself mixed up with them?'

If I could have told him, I'd have told myself.

'I was friends with Emily Cooper.'

'Yes. That was dreadful. I only saw her once. She looked very fey and frail.'

'But she was tough, too. Odd man out. So they wrung her neck like they would a hen's. I went to see her nearly every day. Mostly she was high-spirited; full of fun. I just don't know why . . . I can't understand . . . If only I'd realised . . . She was so intelligent . . . '

'Poor lamb,' Bernard said again.

'I mean, I know why she did it . . . oh . . . sorry . . . I'm not making sense.'

'But you are. That's the point. People like her should never get born into that society. It's dwindling, you see, so all the members have to be counted and kept in line. What a fuck-up.'

'Anyway, she was the only person one could speak to here. It's harsh.'

Thanking him for the lovely afternoon, I went towards the door, concocting visions of bleak loneliness ahead, but when I settled into the trap on top of the pile of timber, he smiled up at me:

'Drop round and keep an old man from going to sleep.'


I worked late that evening in the field, slotting and assembling the jumps, and the following morning myself and the lad hurled whitewash over them with the abandon of firemen.

And at lunch, O'Hagan, my rival, came. The cook's namesake (relation), he came from the dining room, having lunched with 'the quality'. He came full of self-importance. His hair was the colour of rhubarb and he had pink freckles, and the Hon. Mrs Hermione Travers said with a suave smile: 'You two will have to sort things out.'

He called Mrs Travers 'Desdemona' behind her back. He tried to control the attractive Northern vowel sounds by superimposing an upper-class drawl, which he mismanaged, and I laughed, oh so silently.

He slyly tried to find my weak points, flirting one minute, sneering the next, until I lost my temper and told him I was busy and I'd speak to him later; I lost a point, and he realised it, too.

Still fuming internally, when Mrs Travers came out to the yard I blew up. I threatened to leave if they gave him the rides in the gymkhana after all my hard work. Oh, angel of anger!

It made things awkward for them. O'Hagan was working in a racing stables and had only got a couple of days off for the gymkhana, and if I left he wouldn't be able to do the horses for the rest of the holidays. But they still thought they'd break me down. Mrs Travers and I screamed at each other like fishwives and I ended up bursting into tears.

There was no one I could appeal to. Lady Girvan was too remote . . . only Emily . . . but Emily . . . Even if she could come back to defend me, they'd only laugh in her face.

That night I roamed the roads on my bike, unable to face Girvan town, unable to be in the castle, unable to face myself. In bed I tossed and tossed.

A donkey brayed.

Perhaps it will rain and the gymkhana will be cancelled.

I wondered how many people in this house were also awake and had heard the donkey. I thought of Lord and Lady Girvan's enormous bedroom, facing south; it smelled of eau de cologne and nightdresses. I thought of the small cells in which the servants slept in the part of the house with which I was most familiar, and how, in the mornings, I would rush past the doors, sickened by the odour of closed windows, stale clothes and urine, and how everything was geared from six o'clock onwards to the cooking and cleaning for that solitary couple and this new set of pigs who 'took their time' and changed their clothes half a dozen times a day, and how they strolled around like characters from grand opera in those beautifully proportioned rooms, with their high cornices, intricately carved, and how the air in the rooms was fresh and smelled of flowers, and the Chippendale and Sheraton furniture smelled of mansion polish. And how the Spode and Crown Derby china and Waterford glass caught and reflected rays of light and how the lace mats splintered on the mahogany dining table. And I thought of the walls, the Regency wallpaper, the damask curtains, the nineteenth-century landscapes, the Angry Faces of Ancestors, my antlered friends, the scenes of thunder and lightning and sinking ships.

Then I thought of a poster pinned up with drawing pins on a door that needed a lick of paint and I heard the donkey bray again.

Perhaps it won't rain, after all . . . I drifted into sleep.

# 13

And they all came to the lawn to watch the gymkhana.

Julie de Vraie stood at the edge of the field. She watched O'Hagan mount the thoroughbred mare, adjust the leathers, her leathers, to his length. Watched his brown boots flapping on the saddle flaps; flap flap, as he cantered into the first fence.

And Des Mooney came to watch; he carried a flat half-bottle of John Jameson whiskey in the pocket of his jacket. And hoards of local people came and sat about, dropping cigarette cartons and sweet papers. And Julie watched the Hon. Mrs Hermione Travers watching O'Hagan, with her smile and her picture hat. And when it was all over, people scattered like rain showers, leaving the field dappled with litter, and Julie took a swig out of Des' bottle and with nary a word to anyone bedded down the horses for the night and, with half a dozen people from Girvan, got into the town's only taxi.

'How are ye doin', blossom?'

'I thought ye would be riding in the jumping.'

The car drove slowly past the walkers; those who came to have a yearly peep at the big house. It drove past the visiting horses, mostly jogging home in pairs. The strollers stared and stared with eyes of stone: old women, peaky-looking brats, men in wellington boots, young lassies in red dresses and frizzed-up hair.

And later, some hours later: 'Goodnight childe, little chickadee.'

Des Mooney packed a drunken girl into the taxi, the same taxi, dumping a pound note in the driver's hand.

'Drop her off outside the castle.'

The car drives off. I stagger. A penchant for brandy, yes, I have.

Snag is, it makes me sick.

Violently.

> 'Will you walk down the road a bit?'
> 'Will you walk a little faster,'
> Says the whiting to the snail.
> 'Come here you crazy creature.'

'I can't see anything. Is that . . . Bernard?'

'Here!' A hand. And a voice ignited with humour. 'Here!'

And I am being kissed. Kissed many times, very fast. I am drunk.

Definitely drunk. Yes, I must be definitely very drunk.

And that was happiness.

We moved and swayed and kissed. And kissed. We moved and kissed and moved into a gateway. A fieldgate. We kissed into a gateway. We leaned against the iron bars and kissed. We stood, moving always. Kissing.

It must have been he who opened the gate, nicked the piece of wire over the upright spar, shoved me through into the field. I remember. I remember tripping in the ankle-deep holes made and remade by restless beasts. Beasts crowding to get out. To get in. And then, yes, we were on the ground, and I got frightened. That was when I got frightened. I pushed him away. 'No . . . no . . . please . . . '

'The child crying in the wind, to the will-o'-the-wisp: "Don't chase me!"'

And then, in terror, folding up like a sheet.

'No . . . no . . . please . . . '

And my mind is doing something. The mind with its tired

logic of cause and effect. This must not happen because it brings ruin. And what is that?

'What is it? What are you afraid of?'

'I . . . it's the first time. There was another time nearly.'

'Ambiguous statement,' the funny man grunted.

'I was thirteen. Years ago.'

'Go on!'

'He was Spanish. Brown. Beautiful. He was twenty!'

'Heavens above!'

Childish phrases jolting out . . .

'I was five. Lying over the edge of the Cliffs of Moher. The wave-crests were so far away. Like seagulls. And then in Trinity I was thirteen and I thought he might, and I said to myself if he does I'll throw myself over the cliffs. Yes. That was it. And I will.'

'I'll take care of you. I won't make you pregnant. Is that it? I promise.'

'Promises are like charity. Useless.' I began to cry.

And I wanted to say 'Let's just kiss', but I couldn't because I wanted to please. You can't say things like that. It's never like that. All right then. All right.

And afterwards, long afterwards, he slept. Like a cat on the lumpy clay.

And I lay cold, thinking: thank God!

But wake up and kiss me now when I'm alone and the world is crowding back on me.

God knows who might come, and then they'd have words for it.

Disgusting.

Dirty.

'Wake up. Wake up, Bernard. I must go. It's late.'

And all he does is turn and stretch and yawn and say: 'Mmm.'

'Wake up. Wake up.'

'I wish you could stay,' I say, and he says: 'Mmm . . . it would be nice.' And then the last button is being fastened. And the figure is moving away.

The eyes – my eyes – are straining to disentangle the shadows – the figure – the leaves – the ribbon road – the road reflecting the figure – the shadow of the figure, the leaves, the road, the figure in the centre, to the side. Movement. No movement.

# 14

Seeing Nellie's worn-out face at breakfast, I banged on the table with my fist, making the three prissy English girls jump as though a rat had bitten them.

'Damn it. I'll do that.' I took the tray, weighed down with scalding plates, and shoved her on to her chair. With my cuff over my hand, I edged the dishes in front of each servant in turn and then I went into the kitchen and fetched the teapot; I walked round splashing magnolia-coloured tea into everyone's mug. Then I sat down myself and wolfed my food, talking with my mouth full:

'It's time everybody realised that Nellie is overworked.' Silence reared up like an arch.

'Right!' I said. 'From now on, after I've mucked out the stables and tackled the horses, I'm coming back in to share Nellie's chores. You can give me the greasy pans for starters.'

Everyone looked in consternation in the direction of the front part of the house, as if the Germans were on the lawn.

'Has O'Hagan gone yet?' I asked Tom.

'His train goes at twelve,' said the stupefied butler.

'Good. That'll be one less.'

I smiled secretly. I could now apologise to Mrs Travers for being so rude and go back to square one, or square sixty-nine, or whatever square I was at when she arrived.

But my plans went awry.

That morning I was told that I had to begin coaching the young child, Jennifer, in the art of horsewomanship, so, by the time I'd finished with the tiny terrified creature, Nellie had completed most of the scullery work.

I was raging.

I forced her to sit down and have a morning cup of tea.

Tom came in and found us both cracking jokes and he let rip.

'What makes you think you can disrupt the whole household with your newfangled notions?'

Wouldn't you like to know, just? I thought, but I said: 'You know as well as I do that if Nellie gets too ill to work, you'll be banjaxed.' He said nothing but flew out like a madman on roller skates.

Nellie's round face and tangled country-girl hair, clipped in with a slide, her long apron and rolled-up sleeves, her shapeless body leaning back on the wooden chair, was like a sepia photograph of all the servants of the world, hopeful, helpful, hopeless and without hope of help from any quarter whatever.

'You will tell me, Nellie,' I said, 'when there's anything I can do.'

'It's all right, miss. I can manage.'

I took her chin in my two hands and ran my fingers down her neck.

'The swelling's gone, isn't it?'

'Aye,' she said, twisting her face away.

There was no protuberance.

'What's the matter, Nellie? Do they know?'

'The lady says I'm to have treatment when the children go back. In the infirmary.'

'The infirmary?'

No. That terrible opaque building. Not there.

It was once the poorhouse and stood as it was in a treeless field.

When I came first, a man had 'taken bad'. One of the older labourers. He'd been carried out of the field on a door and that's where he'd gone. He died three days later. His name came into my mouth, now, like spittle: Mr Dagg.

'You're wanted in the yard!' Tom, back again, to nag, to interfere.

And God, didn't the afternoon drag!


Bernard was swinging on his chair like a pirate when I went into his kitchen.

'The loud English voices are booming and baying.'

'I was hoping you'd come.'

I could not fathom this articulate man, who was so sophisticated and yet so gentle. And so aloof, as if nothing had happened the previous night!

I told him about my day, about Nellie, about Mrs Travers and how she wanted to oust me from any perks I might get from my job; that I had capitulated weakly.

'People like you will always be in a state of turmoil. You can't play the hypocrisy game because you're too honest, so the "they" you talk about will always try to crack you. You see, we have to tell lies to please people and save our skins.'

' "They" don't.'

'There's more of "them" than you.'

'And that's why Nellie's sick and Emily died?'

'Yes, my pet. Here!'

Agitated, I was pulled over to him.

'I like the way you move. I like the way your pupils swoon when I talk to you. I like your thin bones.'

Gerry was in town, he said. He said he would kiss me and make me warm if I went upstairs with him.

And before I knew where I was, I was in his bed.

And afterwards, amid small intimate bursts of laughter, he fell asleep and actually snored and I (poor me) had to get up and face home on my bike in the middle of the impenetrable night.

Gerry was in the kitchen and I was embarrassed to have him see me creep downstairs.

But, 'Is the old man asleep?' he said, unselfconsciously.

101

'Fast,' I said, not without irony.

'I'd better go,' I said. 'Because of the lord.'

> The Lord's my . . . y . . . she . . . e . . . pherd
> I'll not want. He leadeth me . . .

'Shh!' he said, giggling.

'I've joined the Girvan Dram Soc,' he said.

'I had the notion once. Has Mrs Howard raped you yet?'

Gerry giggled again. '*In pastures green he leadeth . . .* '

'How is it you know a Protestant hymn if you're at Clongowes?'

'I have Protestant connections on the stock exchange.'

'You're very nice,' I said impulsively.

After drinking tea with him, I forced myself to head for the castle. He walked me all the way down to the road, swinging the storm lantern and singing as ever: '*Oh God our help in ages past . . .* ' But at the gate he switched off his flippant mood: 'Mind how you go on that lousy bike. And you won't get the sack.'

As I once said to Nellie, Gerry said to me. Whether going up or down the scale, I must jump on to the bicycle and ride, lonely into the night.

# 15

And all this time I had done nothing in my mind about Nicholas. Nothing at all. Occasionally, static visions, like lantern slides, of himself and Nancy in the sitting room of the house in Lansdowne Road flashed in front of my eyes. That was all. He had not written to me and I, having immediately become so involved with the intricate mosaic of life in Girvan, after that first childish communication had not put pen to paper either.

I suddenly thought of him now, while I cycled in frantic haste along the side road that lead to Bernard's house. Hurling my machine into the haggard, I walked up Bernard's boreen, still thinking of him, wondering would he help me ever. Ever help me to escape. The end of the summer; the end of my job was like a car hanging over the edge of a cliff. Any move at all might be fatal.

I found Bernard and said: 'When my job ends here, I'll have to go to England.'

'Being both mysterious and dramatic.'

'Not really. For once practical. I have a cousin.'

'So have I.'

'Bernard, be serious!'

'I am extremely serious.'

He spun me round like a gyroscope on a string till I pirouetted between his knees. He ran his hands up the inside of my shirt and said: 'Why are brassieres so difficult to undo?'

'Pity I can't get a phrase book that gives you an answer to all these questions.'

'Now who's not serious?'

'And my cousin's name is Nicholas.'

My pupils swooned from his gaze, fearful I was pushing things. He looked compassionate at first and then, strangely, incomprehensibly, sad.

I laid my head against him, my hair brushing his chin, my fingers kneading the wool of his pullover.

He jerked my head backwards by my hair and began kissing me; long stormy kisses. He pushed me up and dragged me across the kitchen and shoved me back against the wall. I began to cry. It was all so crazy.

'Well,' he said. 'You're crying now. You'll cry more later.'

He picked me up and stumbled up the stairs. He chucked me on the bed and, taking his trousers off, pulled my pants down and began jumping up and down on me.

'You're going to do it,' I screamed.

'Oh, get off that old tack.'

'I can't stand it,' I said.

'You'll stand it,' he said, his voice furious. Then, with a long groan, he leapt away from me.

Left abandoned, I went on sobbing.

He raised himself on one elbow: 'Tears don't become you. But I'm sorry, sorry. Sorry, darling.' He pulled up the bedclothes, gently covering me; he stroked my eyebrows with one finger: 'Beware of whose eyebrows meet,' he said. 'I don't know why I did that. It wasn't very subtle. I ought to have known better. Are you happy here?'

'Yes.'

'Then let's forget it. Tell me one thing: is he here?'

'No, he's over there in England.'

I started to tell him that Nicholas, as a person, didn't concern me, but he said: 'No explanations.'

Later, much later, we went downstairs, holding each other. I touched him while he lit the Primus, took out the inevitable rashers, watched them curl and spatter as he lifted them with the fork.

Not leaving his body, I stretched for the eggs. We ate sitting side by side.

'This is becoming a ritual. This bacon and eggs. Do you like it?'

'Yes.'

'Were you brought up a Protestant?' I asked him one night.

This seemingly naive question didn't make him laugh as I was afraid it might.

'I believe I was baptised one.'

'And did your parents not force you to church?'

'They may have, before I was four.'

'They died?'

'The idiots went out in a sailing boat on a wet day.'

'That was sad.'

'Not really. I don't remember them. So, consequently, I was brought up rough.'

'That was lucky. Wish I had. I always wanted to be an orphan. But I got stuck with living parents. Except for my ma. She died a year ago.'

'Oh, there was nothing romantic or Dickensian about my upbringing. A very pleasant and liberal aunt brought up myself and my three brothers and one sister. We lived in a faintly humorous house in the country near Omagh.'

'So anyway,' I persisted, 'you believe it's all a lie.'

'Probably. But for some, obviously, a very necessary one.'

'I'm terrified of God. I have to cross the road when I see a clergyman coming.'

'When you think of the effort one puts into living, it's a bore to think one has only one life. But there's nothing, as far as I can see, to be done about it.'

'What about Jesus Christ and all that?'

'What's to stop me getting up and addressing Girvan and saying I'm the new Messiah? If I had the energy.'

'You'd be signed on immediately for the Dram Soc. Could I be your dresser?'

'The only snag is your bishop's son would have me burnt for a heretic. Martyrdom's not my line.'

'But seriously, I'm still afraid. I'd like to think there was some place for Emily. She'd go to heaven, if there is one.'

'Julie, Julie,' Bernard said. 'Emily, your beloved Emily lived in a cold, cold place, and that's why it seems so much worse; makes the tragedy so immediate. You must forget your wound while remembering her. You're one of the innocents, and that she should have a place in the minds of the innocents is more than most of us can hope for after we leave this orb.'

'But the Protestants all hated her. Just like they hate me.'

'I know, pet.'

'That's all very well, but what am I going to do? I can't stay looking after horses all my life. And what's England, only wiping grit off a window-pane; staring out at life? I can't communicate with these people. If I ever once said the right thing at the right time, my way would be smooth as silk. But I don't know the formula.'

'Do you imply I do?'

'You know it hell of a lot better than me.'

'I'm more than twice your age.'

'Does experience make any difference? I'd like to think there was some hope.'

'One of your troubles is that you chase happiness with such a frenzy, you haven't time to stop suffering.'

'Christ, Bernard, you make it sound bleak.'

'Bleak it is,' he said. 'My formula is to keep out of the way of such people you're always listing. Otherwise . . . Otherwise you'll come back one day and find the place deserted. Like the *Marie Celeste*. Table laid, beds turned down, but no occupants anywhere. Choose your occupants. And that's all the advice you're getting from Uncle Bernard. You'd better stay the night. You're in a bad way.'

So it came to that. Half of the time I didn't go home at all. The evenings were unendurably short; far too short to encompass the pleasure they contained. Bernard loved music. And I learned names like Prokofiev, de Falla, Stravinsky, Granados. He had a stack of wax records and an old EMG with a horn. He told me about people called Jean Cocteau, Modigliani, Apollinaire, and how they lived, as an example of the different ways in which genius chooses to destroy itself. Sometimes Gerry accompanied us till we went to bed, but when we were alone there was always something to say. I used to sneak in about a quarter to eight, dash up to my bedroom, ruffle the bed and dash back down to breakfast.

He never asked me about Nicholas, or my plans; never spoke about his personal past or future; only talked about his 'trade'.

My position at the castle was, as ever, tense and tenuous. I knew they'd get rid of me when the children went back to school. As regards my job, I had nothing to look forward to except the annual Girvan show, which I hoped would not be such a fracas as the gymkhana at the castle; I continued to school the animals and teach the children, keeping as far from the aura of their mother, Mrs Travers, as was possible. The group hatred from below-stairs was at full rein; apart from Nellie, they drove their knives in my back.

Yet the tired, disillusioned Nellie kept saying: 'Let them talk, they're jealous.'

In the mornings, Brennen would throw up the window, his plucked duck's neck extended maliciously through the aperture, and would announce the exact time of my passing the previous evening.

I was called a brazen hussy and that I had no shame.

'There she goes. And on a boy's bike, too.'

PART IV

# 16

Dearest Julie,

Have had an enormous piece of luck. The whole outfit's being shifted further North to get away from the V Bombs. The unit's being temporarily disbanded, so redundant pedants like myself are being let off the hook for an unexpected week. I've booked myself into a pub called the Hibernian, I expect you know it? So you'd better meet me Tuesday evening about 7 o'clock. If I'm out, I'll leave a message.

Have been thinking about you,

Yours ever,
Nicholas

The note was addressed to Girvan Castle; the family grapevine must have circulated my whereabouts.

That evening, I rapped on the drawing-room door.

'Come in; don't hover in the doorway.'

'I've come to ask you . . . Er . . . I've had a letter from my cousin in England . . . '

'Well, what is it?'

Lord Girvan turned the wick of the Aladdin up and down till the mantle purred favourably with its green-yellow glow.

'Yes, that's what I've come for. Sorry to disturb you.'

Lord Girvan looked at Lady Girvan as if questioning her as to the reason for the rotting smell. I plunged.

'Could I possibly have the next few days off to go to Dublin?'

It was like the last gallop before the water jump.

Lady Girvan settled back into her chair, her black garments folding downwards like the open pages of a book.

In spite of everything, I had a sneaking admiration for Lady Girvan. In the early days, I'd tried to get to know her; there were traces of humour in her face, signs that the serious business of being upper class had not made her entirely inhuman, and I gambled on this.

But, to my disappointment, Lady Girvan looked out of the window as if I wasn't there.

There was a lamentable silence. A silence in which Lord Girvan rustled the *Irish Times* and Lady Girvan sighed audibly.

Then: 'You want the week off?'

I muttered something, ready to run.

And Lord Girvan began. He listed, categorised and dated all my misdemeanours since my arrival. He used words like 'undesirable', 'unsuitable', 'untrustworthy', awkwardly ping-ponging the phrases one to the other while I stood defeated in the doorway.

And then, when he'd finished, he coldly said I could have the next few days off, and after I came back: 'He'd see.'


I was shattered. I yelled for Nellie, who made me a cup of tea. I told her I was being let off the hook for a few days, and Nellie said it was a miracle.

Nellie had waited in Dublin for the Girvan bus; she had wandered into O'Connell Street, seen the neon lights, the cheap cafés; for one hour, she'd been a part of the fairyland and tension of the city.

'I'd love to go with you,' she said.

## 17

I must have cut a figure, all right, pedalling down the back avenue of Girvan Castle; I was wearing a flowered cotton dress and high-heeled shoes, and my overcoat was folded over the handlebars; my cracked fibre suitcase bounded off the ground as I pushed into Girvan.

There was no car in Bernard's front driveway. I ran up the steps and hammered on the door.

'Hang on!' Gerry, the casuist, deliberately sane, said: 'Where are you off to?'

'Where's Bernard?'

'I don't know. Can't be gone long.' He scrutinised me. 'What's up?'

'Nothing.'

'I just have to finish something,' Gerry said. 'Why don't you go in and light the Primus?'

I fidgeted around the kitchen. The kettle began to boil. Everything was quiet and normal except for the fact that Bernard wasn't there. As I was about to make the tea, frissons of panic overtook me. If he did come in, what was I going to say to him? What if he was indifferent?

The lady in the Modigliani poster was indifferent. Gerry, humming away upstairs, was indifferent. The clutter of saucepans, the empty stout bottles and the friendly boiling kettle were indifferent. I closed my hand over the knob of the Primus and it hissed to a stop. I'd been running round in circles, chasing God knew what, and the whole world was indifferent. I ran into the glaring sunshine, jumped on my bike and went *bump bump bump* down the cart-track till my overcoat caught in the front wheel and clogged in the mudguard and I rolled off and fell into the dust. I ripped and pulled at the garment till it was free, and with coat and suitcase and bicycle I ran on, out on to the road, mounted and pedalled like fury, past Brennen's, past the few smallholdings, on to the main road, under the railway bridge, and free-wheeled on to Main Street, crashing against the window of Des Mooney's shop.

And Des Mooney laughed and said: 'What in the name of God?'

'I have to catch the bus.'

'It doesn't go till five. You're in a desperate way.'

He locked the shop and led me into the pub.

'I haven't seen you for a long long time,' he said in the dark interior. 'Where have you been?'

I glared into my Cairn's ale and he glared into his stout.

'Around.'

'Like hell you have.'

'Oh, the whiskey,' I said after a silence.

'What whiskey?'

'The whiskey you bought me at the gymkhana. That saved my bacon.'

He seemed to have forgotten but he said, vaguely: 'All in a day's work.'

I asked him the time; he didn't reply, and when, a while later, I asked him the time again, he rose from the bar-stool, saying: 'Here! You'd better have this for the journey.' It was his folded *Independent*.

As the bus went grumbling up Main Street to turn at the top, I said: 'I don't want to go.'

'Don't go, then.'

At the bus stop, I said: 'I'm sorry.'

# 18

The Dublin bus bowled along. The tarpaulins thundered on the roof.

The thin wispy villages, attuned to the passing of this human meteor, slumbered, indifferent, in the heat. Julie de Vraie was crushed beside boxes, heavy women, children, sharp-faced and smelling of smoke, and as the drab terrain gave way to thicker grass, greener trees, her metabolism gradually changed: she was on the move, for better or worse.

She got off at the halfway stop, where everyone piled into the pub. It was cool in the jacks, with the thin trickle of brown water in the basin and the chain that didn't pull. Cool, too, in the shop part of the pub, where mothers purchased lemonade and kids whined for sweets.

'Pennorth of bull's eyes, mister.'


'Are you sure?' Julie begged the clerk at the reception desk.

'He doesn't answer.'

'Is there no message?'

The clerk flicked through a pile of envelopes.

'Nothing,' he said with relief.

She hitched at her suspenders as she entered the lounge. A smattering of wealthy mothers and grown-up children anticipating wealthy men studied the pages of *Country Life*. Julie, anticipating nothing, sat down on the chintz-covered chair and her skirt rode up her thighs.

Hell!

She summoned a waitress.

'Can I have a cup of tea, please.'

'Afternoon tea?'

The clock said quarter past eight.

'Can I have a drink, then, please?'

'Drinks are served below in the buttery.'

Nicholas greeted Julie as if she was his exclusive property.

'I checked on the bus. It should have been there quite some time ago.' He brushed her hair with his lips. 'I thought you'd missed it. I'll get you a drink.'

'Can I have a brandy, please.'

The faces around the bar all looked as if they belonged to 'someone'.

'What are you reading?' Julie asked Nicholas, her eyes on the book tucked under his arm.

'A turgid tome on biology.'

'Not *Gray's Anatomy*?' Julie looked at the faces, hoping they'd hear her and think her 'someone'.

'That's pre-med stuff.'

After the second drink, she began again. She pushed against the bar and her hair hung down in strings.

'How's the war?'

'Undeniably boring for me. Not so nice for the Londoners.'

'I've had an awful summer,' Julie said.

'You must tell me all about it.'

And Julie began to ramble on. After he'd picked up her hand and dropped it a few times and stifled the occasional yawn, it occurred to her that she might be going on a bit. She held out her empty glass for more but he took it and placed it on the counter.

'Hmm . . . ' he said. 'Do you know where to eat? I'm a bit out of touch.'

In Dawson Street, she was spinning like a top.

'I remember a place . . . it's probably terrible.'

It was a quaint, over-decorated restaurant. A stuffed fox mounted between two hunting prints hung from the facing wall.

'Home from home,' Julie said, as the waiter held her chair.

'No wine licence?' Nicholas read the menu.

Julie dreaded a scene.

'I thought there were no shortages in Ireland.'

'Only tea and sugar.'

'Will I send out for beer, sir?'

'Don't bother.'

They ordered and ate in silence.

'Not exactly piquant!' Nicholas drummed on the tablecloth.

Luckily the waiter's face betrayed nothing except the impassivity of his calling, and Nicholas' temper improved after eating. He got up and stretched, running his long, pointed fingers down his silk shirt, which corrugated his ribs.

'Come, my dear.'

As if the fates were stacked, in the first pub they tried, the publican declared, in a whisper, that no ladies were allowed.

'It's not the end of the world,' Nicholas said, guiding Julie out again.

So they went back down Dawson Street, in search of more liberal publicans.

'Now, my dear, you can tell me more about your associates since you've joined the earldom.'

'Joined?' Julie said, stubbornly silent once more.

'Environmental acquaintances can be quite rewarding.' Nicholas was relentless.

'Well, Emily Cooper. She was my friend.'

'A fellow worker?'

'No, no, forget about it.'

'You don't seem very enthusiastic about your employers. They can't be that bad. I don't especially like my superior officers; in fact, I find them excessively stupid. But one jogs along. Anyway, what have you done?'

'It's just that they don't approve of me, and Emily Cooper's dead. She was mad! Lord Girvan's cousin.'

'She committed suicide?'

'Can I have more brandy, please?' Julie petulantly waved her bell-like glass upside down between two of her fingers.

'I'm not a millionaire,' Nicholas laughed, but he bought her another drink.

'Anyway,' Julie said, 'I'm beginning to forget, I think.'

'Unfortunately, when you meet a person like that for the first time, you get an unreal feeling of responsibility towards them, and then, when the inevitable tragedy occurs, you think it's your fault.'

'That's how it was.'

'But it's not, you know.' Julie looked into her glass.

'Come on!'

'Oh, I know, but she wasn't just *that* sort of person; she was strange, uncertain, intelligent. But what got me down was that they ignored all this. Anyway, as I said, I'm trying to forget, so tell me about your life for a change.'

Nicholas remained sympathetic for a while but when Julie's laughter got a shade loud, he had doubts again. He told her he had to meet a friend and looked at her, his mouth rolled up like an olive.

Julie, in a panic, said: 'Can I come with you? Who are you meeting?'

'Old Benjamin's not the worst. All right then, you can come along. He's got a new Czech wife. He's a physics lecturer. We were at the London School of Slavonic Studies together. He'd done physics at Cambridge when I was reading history. We're sort of inside-out colleagues.'

'I suppose you speak Czech?'

'I speak Serbo-Croat and Russian.'

Julie followed Nicholas, tripping occasionally, trying to seem sober, to the appointed bar.

Holding the door, Nicholas said: 'You'd better have a coffee first. Benjamin's all right but hmm . . . '

'How old is old Benjamin?'

'Not ninety. We are, give or take a few years, contemporaries. When Trinity offered him a job, he decided to take it; it killed two birds with one stone. He'd avoid the war and eat simultaneously.'

# 19

Julie was startled at the sight of Benjamin. He was bald, with a floating beard. He also had a fluted voice. Every time he laughed, which was constantly, he hitched his trousers; he tapered away like an ice-cream cone.

Katya, on the other hand, was firmly square; she had a mathematically accurate fringe which fell to her eyebrows.

'Charmed,' Benjamin puffed, as he took Julie's hand. 'What beautiful fingers.' And, turning her hand palm-upwards, said: 'I can't tell you what I see here!'

He chuckled as he looked at Nicholas: 'Where did you find this gorgeous creature with such an execrable future in store for her? You old devil!'

Nicholas said he didn't know Benjamin indulged in palmistry.

'It's fascinating,' Benjamin said, lengthening his vowels.

Katya cut in: 'He finks he's a clairvoyant . . . Madame Benjamine . . . '

The party was getting quickly into its stride.

Benjamin singled Julie out. 'We'll let the old people get on with it.' He snuffled in her ear.

Julie began to unburden herself to Benjamin, who said things like: 'How can people be such monsters?'

'Nicholas thinks I'm being silly.'

'Ha, the eternal student. He thinks too much.' He was delighted to find a flaw in Nicholas's perfection. 'Besides, he is afraid of you.'

'Are you dreaming?'

'Of course not. All old men are afraid of young girls. I'm afraid of you.'

'You wouldn't say it if you were,' Julie said, diffidently.

There was silence in the strangling noise; a pocket of embarrassed silence between her and Benjamin. Her thoughts strayed to Bernard, so far from this pub, so solid, but Benjamin was effusive, and determined to track her down.

'What are you thinking about?' he squeaked. 'I know, you need another drink.'

'Yes. I was thinking about how wonderful alcohol is. That's what I was thinking. One minute you're in despair, and the next you're in heaven.'

Julie's spirits began to soar in the brutish glow of Benjamin's flattery. She ignored the identifiable pangs that the sight of Nicholas and Katya, absorbed in some mutual Slavonic tongue, caused her. The more Benjamin drank, the more hyperbolic he became. The quick high decibels, and his infectious giggling, caused a few disapproving glances from strangers. When closing time came, they were transported in a taxi to a bonafide in the Dublin Mountains.

Julie sat between the two men, with Katya on the outside, and as Benjamin held her hand in a greedy clutch, Nicholas put his arm round her and suddenly kissed her. The kissing was voracious, inescapable, and it made Julie extraordinarily excited. His superbly controlled emotional balance was now being violently countermanded. They jostled and fought in the back of the taxi as though Benjamin and Katya weren't there. But the journey ended abruptly and with consequent hubris.

They all piled out, with Benjamin tuffing and huffing. Although the night had been somewhat re-scaled, Julie was unable to find a foothold in the new bright roaring pub; she escaped upstairs and looked at the odd creature in the mirror, whose hair curled inwards over bare collarbones. Her dark uneven features disturbed her; she didn't really like what she saw.

'Should I buy myself gold-hooped earrings in Woolworth's tomorrow?' she asked the reflection.

The three of them now looked disgustingly contented, and Katya, having recently recovered from the most frightful experiences in Europe, was holding Benjamin's arm in a strangely grateful way; their voices were dark and urgent, all three encouraging each other – Katya, too, was a scientist – and Julie tried to spread herself out between them, feeling in a worse void than ever.

The barmen were fulminating, shouting last orders, quickly emptying, rinsing, and filling pints of stout, spirit measures, and pulling corks, and suddenly there was a commotion; people rushed out and surged back in. In a second, the place was filled with gardaí. Giants in navy blue stalked up to the counter. The populace evaporated and the four found themselves amid a cluster of people in a dead village, some singing, some fighting, but none of them with any visible means of transport. An old Ford taxi loomed, and the crowd advanced on the car. Before they could either push back or press forward, the four of them were diving into the vehicle. Others piled in on top, some ran round trying to force the driver's door, and the driver had to exert all his willpower to remove the surplus without having his vehicle turned upside down. They were jam-packed, knees and arms over- and underlapping. A little man with hard, pointed shoes scraped Julie's tendons. She was pushed and kissed by a stranger.

'Stop, stop, stop . . . ' Benjamin, from under a mound of clothing, screamed: 'Don't!'

'Aou, daon't,' someone mimicked.

When Julie came up for air, having with great difficulty unpinned her dress from the lapel of someone's coat, she saw that Nicholas, trust him, was sitting aloof and extremely comfortable in the front seat beside the driver.

Well I'm damned, thought Julie. You miserable bastard!

Benjamin and Katya occupied the hall floor and return of an elegant flat in Merrion Square.

When they were ensconced, Benjamin produced four glasses and a bottle of brandy, and then, pretending to be in deadly earnest, began to gurgle.

It was lunacy.

'We'll play games with the occult,' he squeaked.

Julie, still discomfited by the peripheral part she was playing, hoped the new supply of alcohol would bring on oblivion. She dived into a glass and drank it neat. Benjamin turned out the light and put on the electric fire.

'No, turn that off,' Katya said.

'My dear chap,' said Nicholas.

'The spirits might knock over our spirits before they've improved our spirits,' Julie said. 'Ha ha ha.'

'Ha ha ha ha,' Benjamin gurgled.

Katya pulled the flex out of the wall.

They all began feeling for their drinks, which were on the table that was supposed to jump.

'Ve haf too many unbeliefers, no. Nicholas, you an unbeliefer?'

Nicholas laughed contentedly.

'OK, we'll dance.'

Benjamin jumped up, and the light went on. He wound up an old HMV and selected a dance number. He bowed to Julie.

In the way of most fat men, he danced like an angel. His feet fell like snowflakes on the carpet. Julie tripped and ran to keep up with him while he breathed into her neck with sexy sniffles.

Every time the record had to be changed, Julie took a swig of brandy. She longed to dance with Nicholas but didn't know how to organise this.

Then he got up with Katya and the four of them went flying round, knocking into armchairs, tables, tripping over the carpet and generally creating mayhem. Somewhere in the middle of all this, a stranger, wearing a raincoat and pyjamas, appeared.

He kept repeating that he had to get up in the morning.

They gazed at him with the selfish intensity of drunks, and then Benjamin said: 'Everyone gets up in the morning.'

'English cunts!'

'My dear chap!'

Benjamin squeaked: 'We're friendly aliens.'

'I don't care whether yez are friendly aryans. Or Eyeties.'

He grabbed the needle off the record.

They were chastened and momentarily silenced. Needless to say, when the neighbour had retired, the noise started up again. Everybody began talking at once, intermittently saying: 'Shh . . . '

Julie was beginning to feel integrated, relaxed, when the next moment the room went spinning. Floundering out, she fled up the stairs, dived through the first doorway and, unable to find the light-switch, blindly grabbed a porcelain edge. Up came chicken sandwich, coffee, brandy and all other objects taken in the last few hours. Misery, bitterness, shame and the familiar smell of undigested liquor were all too much for her. She had disgraced Nicholas; she had felt lonely and bored all evening. She sank to the floor in drunken anguish.

# 20

There were birds. Birds . . . birds . . . tweeting. Like a pianola being played too quickly. It was light. They must be little birds. Then there were seagulls. *Cawk.* And this was outside her head. Inside was a blacksmith beating on an anvil, taking his time to make a piece of iron the right shape. Water! Water . . . *clang* . . . *tweet* . . . *cawk* . . . *clang.*

She faced the wall. Blank. Large.

'Come here!'

Julie quickly rolled on to her other side, which caused the blacksmith to miss the anvil and then go *clang clang clang.* There were two beds. Neat as coffins. Nicholas was in the other bed.

'I must have water!'

'The bathroom's just outside.'

'No.'

'Come here.'

'I didn't, did I? Oh God. The bath!'

'In here.' He moved the blankets to show her there was space in the coffin.

She crept into his bed.

'I'm dying.'

'I don't know what's wrong with me. Now that I'm here, it doesn't seem to work.'

Julie wished she could make some lucid statement, but with her nose buried in his collarbone, she said nothing.

'My analyst advises marriage. I'm a bit of a roué, you know.'

He turned sideways to her, tongue in cheek.

'And you're very pretty. *Jolie laide.*'

'More laid than jolly.'

'Hmm . . . '

'Perhaps I should take you back with me and send you to college. I'm quite well off. The King of England seems to think I'm worth paying to speak Russian.'

'Not everyone speaks Russian.'

'It's only monkey business.'

'Oh.' She curled her legs over his.

She was strung up with anticipation. She wanted to jump out of bed and say 'When can we go?' but she was afraid to say anything in case he changed his mind.

But he said no more, just lay on his back with his arm lapped round her shoulder in the most offhand manner.

Then, suddenly: 'You'd better get back into your own bed.'

'No, no!'

'Yes.'

And turning his back, he got into the other bed himself.

Abandoned, Julie began whimpering.

'Behave yourself!'

She got out and in beside him.

'Do what you're told.'

And Nicholas got up and, naked, began to make the other bed. When it was neat, he quietly got in and, with unbiddable tones, said: 'No more musical beds, now! Do you hear me?'

She waited, wondering would he change his mind; she didn't move. The other bed, too, was quiet. At last she plucked up courage and crept out to the bathroom. The bath was brutally clean. That was the end! She thought of the Girvan bus as the one particle of hope in a narrowing world. But her head ached and her bones screamed for rest. She went back to bed and slept.

The sun, like a slave, was determined to please. Part of the room was in raw bright light, the other part in shade. The bed beside her was empty.

Julie dressed and emerged uncertainly.

126

The flat was empty.

Accoutrements for breakfast were laid out for her.

There was no note.

She had no cigarettes.

She searched her handbag, found one scent-sodden Woodbine, drew on it and was nearly sick again.

She paced the sitting room. She turned a miniature buddha this way and that. She could steal this and go to Russia after the war. She could go back to Girvan on her return ticket.

She pressed her forehead against the window-pane.

Outside in the square, the laurel bushes are covered in dust.

I've forgotten my password.

The Primus has hissed to a stop.

A rope! Come quick, milord, sir.

My daughter, Mrs Travers, wants O'Hagan to ride the . . .

There's been a lot of gossip . . .

Why don't you say something . . . say something . . . are you dumb?


'You can't make snap judgements!'

'No. But vere are certain rule by which you can abide.'

'She has an enormously happy disposition,' cut in Benjamin.

They were returning from the pub, rolling along like sailors, oblivious of Julie, discussing her.

Embarrassed, she drew back from the window.

'You categorise, and consequently generalise too much, old boy. You can't rub off familial or environmental contagion overnight. We are cousins, and I feel I know something about her.' Julie wondered why they wanted to discuss anyone so unimportant as her. Probably Benjamin with his boyish curiosity had brought up the subject.

'You like to pigeon-hole people, and when you're not looking they've escaped. Then you have to find somewhere else for them.'

'You think too much for your age,' Benjamin said. 'You're like a schoolboy who's discovered ideas for the first time. Do you remember in King's when we used to sit up all night drinking coffee and solving the riddles of the world? You haven't changed one whit. Look at me! I've learnt sense. I prefer to turn to page 82 and find out what other people have decided.'

'You're a lazy bugger, Benjamin,' Nicholas laughed. 'Ireland has done for you.'


All was bustle in the kitchen. Middle European dishes were being prepared; Katya was determined to surpass herself.

Julie helped wash vegetables and scrub saucepans as sauces boiled up and dried like concrete over the edges.

'I vouldn't tak so much peel off ze potatoes,' Katya said.

Fuck the potatoes, Julie thought, while she obeyed her.

And no mention of the bath!

She was fed up being stuck in the kitchen since she'd been left behind that morning; fed up having to succumb to a behaviour pattern forced on her by Nicholas. But she knew she was being unfair. Katya and Benjamin were delightful, hospitable people, tolerant to a degree; it wasn't their fault if she felt left out. They were right: she *was* stubborn, childish, untutored, and by all standards unreliable.

In this dejected state, she followed Katya into the sitting room with a trayful of succulent food.


'Are we feeling better?' Benjamin asked, all concern.

'I feel all right. That is: terrible! I thought you weren't coming back!'

'And why on earth should you think that?'

'Well, why didn't you tell me which pub you were going to? I could have followed you.'

'We decided to let you sleep,' Nicholas said, biting his bottom lip.

'I needed a drink ever so badly,' Julie said, pettishly.

'We'll cut out a little of the drinking today,' said Nicholas, using his friendly schoolmaster tone.

'I'm going out to see my Uncle Bob – your great-uncle Bob, for that matter – so you can come along.'

Uncle Bob, an old seafarer, grew melons in his garden; his tumbledown house was filled with trophies collected over the years, gods of gilt and stone. He had loved and reared a straggling family, who had gone this way and that, some to the bad, and some to flights of scholarly eccentricity. His elder son, William, had once been married to Nancy, the same Nancy who had helped to sew 'freedom' inside Julie's shirt.

And Julie asked, hopefully: 'Will Nancy be there?'

'Alas, no,' Nicholas said. 'She is in the North, working in some tiresome government office.'

'What a shame.'

While Nicholas talked to this beloved man, Julie ran down the lane, where a man had recently disposed of the butchered remains of his mother, and plunged into the icy sea.

The round pebbles, bruising the instep, the white horses, heaving and falling, the blues, the greens and purples of Bray Head, juxtaposed by the dirty white cliffs along Killiney beach, did a great deal to clear the alcoholic refuse of the previous night.

Julie was mesmerised by the repetition, the spray crashing on the stones and dragging the pebbles back, for ever and ever, using, abusing, refreshing; the Egyptian saying: 'Death is in this place; make it new.'

She hurled a stone far out into the green-blue depths. One more pebble will make no difference, she thought, as she got up to go back.

# 21

A gramophone blared and a deaf man jogged up and down in time to the music.

> Girl of a million dreams
> You have a million charms
> And every night, I turn out the light
> And find you are in my arms . . .

Julie and Nicholas were in the passage of a small suburban house near Sandymount.

There was a narrow staircase.

'Una says we can have the blue room . . . ha ha . . . '

'Oh, goodness.'

'My goodness me!'

'Where's the light?'

' 'Sno light. Bulb's broken. Una's very kind.'

'Is it kind to put girls in bed with ruthless men?'

'Very very kind.'

'There's no room here.'

There was a box with a bed in it. The light was dim red.

' 'Slike a brothel.'

There were orange wine bottles on the wallpaper.

'It's a blue room. Ha ha ha.'

'Must have been blue once. Orange now.'

'It's lovely.'

Nicholas took off Julie's shoes. They tumbled on the bed.

'That's better.'

Half-dressed, they curled up, kissed, fell asleep. They woke up, kissed again.

'Are you awake?'

'Mmm . . . '

'Will you marry me? I'm a bit fucked up. Did I tell you?'

'In Merrion Square.'

'Not only in Merrion Square. In Yugoslavia as well.'

'D'you like Tito?'

'Sh . . . As I was saying. Did I say?'

'Yes. In Merrion Square.'

'Yes. I suppose it's my mum's fault.'

'What did she do?'

'That's what my analyst's trying to find out.'

'Do you lie on the couch with your eyes shut?'

'I mostly write cheques, which my analyst cashes. We have a fulsome relationship.'

'And is he getting down to brass tacks?'

'Oh well, they know a bit, don't you know.' Nicholas was now fully awake, lying in his favourite position, his hands clasped underneath his head.

'So what way does your being fucked up take you?'

'I have a penchant for little girls.'

'Very small ones?'

'They come in all sizes.'

'Oh.'

'But you I might marry.'

'You might.' And Julie began to cry.

'I ask someone to marry me and they burst into tears.'

'It's an experiment.' Julie sobbed.

'You see, I can't just go round grabbing schoolgirls!'

'Why not? And leave me in peace. I've left school.'

Julie turned her back and pressed her forehead against the wall.

'Come here. One should never talk about sex in bed.' And he pulled her round and kissed her. After the war! The things that are going to happen after the war!

131

But in the depth of the bed, there was touching and warmth and they both fell asleep.

In the hour before dawn, when all matter seems to be suspended, Nicholas rose and, dressing quietly, crept out of the little house.

# 22

Una had sent the children out to play. She sat, badly hungover, in the dirty kitchen, alone. She sat there a long time, then she went up to the blue room. It was empty. She went into her own room and woke up her husband. She opened and shut her mouth many times. Dennis laughed, shrugged his shoulders, laughed again.

'I'll get up,' he said softly, as most deaf men do.

> A few hours of gladness
> And then comes the dawn
> I wake with sadness
> And find you are gone . . .

Sandymount Avenue is a long windy road. The early-morning noises had begun . . . the seagulls, round the bins . . . *cawk*. Sea smells, garbage, a lonely cyclist.

Julie felt great. Still drunk. She walked towards the sea.

It was very far away. Near Howth Head.

She jumped over the wall and walked along the sand. Sand. Sand. And mud. Seabirds swooped, flew away when she approached, glided on the wind. The wind was cold, exhilarating. Julie ran on the muddy sand and her heels sank in. She took off her shoes and ran towards the sea. She waded through the channels, puddles. The sun came up and reflected on the mirror of the watery strand. Julie lifted her skirt and ran into the ripples, ran, ran, ran, till the salt stung her thighs. She ran back, undressed and ran out again, till at last the shallows dipped and she swam. She swam till she was out of her depth and the Martello tower was like a sandcastle in the distance. She trod the icy water, turned and swam back towards the shore.

She picked up her clothes and ran till the wind dried her out. She dressed, ran towards the road. She ran towards the dirty little house she'd just left. She rang. Knocked, rang, went round the back. The place was empty. It was spotlessly clean. She opened the kitchen door and went in.

'Are you sure?'

'He doesn't answer.'

It was a different clerk; shift work.

The lounge was empty and smelled of floor polish. A vacuum cleaner hummed. A huge man came rushing into the hall, grabbed his bag and went out into Dawson Street. The clerk read the *Independent*.

Julie went into Dawson Street; it was desolate. Lots of people. Desolate.

She walked into South Anne Street, turned right at Grafton Street and went into Mitchell's. She counted her money and then read the menu.

'Tea. A pot of tea, please.'

'No, thanks. Nothing else.'

'Try again, please.'

The clerk looked at Julie and went back to the racing page.

'Will you have him paged?'

The clerk picked up the intercom and said 'Page Mr Taylor,' then went back to the racing page.

Julie picked her nails.

She went into the lounge and opened the *Irish Times*.

Winston Churchill had made another rousing speech. There was a picture of the German ambassador entertaining at a garden party.

Julie got up. She had the sense of loss that holds out no hope at all. She went out into Dawson Street. Walked up and into St Stephen's Green. It was all gleaming with flowers and ducks and people in summer clothes. It was after twelve. It was very hot. She sat in a deckchair and then, when the ticket man came, she got up and lay on the grass. She shut her eyes.

It was three o'clock. She was all wet. She had a blinding headache. She flopped down Dawson Street. She stopped and bought aspirin.

'Did he leave a message?'

'He said he'd be here at five.'

She went back to Mitchell's.

'A pot of tea, please.'

'No, nothing else, thank you.'

'Can I have a packet of four Woodbines?'

'We only sell them in tens.'

'Ten woodbines, then, please.'

'We've no Woodbines left. Only Players and Kerry Blues.'

'Ten Kerry Blue, please.'

She opened the packet. The cigarettes were mouldy.


'I wonder would you dry these out for me?'

The clerk looked at the packet of fags. He looked at the girl. He sniggered. He called the boots. The boots was three foot six. The clerk leaned right out of his cubicle.

'Dry the young lady's cigarettes!'

The boots sniggered.

Julie watched the boots disappear towards, she supposed, the kitchen, where, she supposed, he would bake them. She always baked them herself; it was quite simple. She hoped he wouldn't roast them.

She tried hard not to laugh.

'About time!'

'Let's go and have a drink.'

Julie's stomach was full of tea.

'What have you been doing all day?'

'I went out to Naas to see Geoffrey Arnold.'

'I thought he was dead.'

'It's his grand-nephew.'

'How interesting.'

'Did you have a nice day, too?'

'Marvellous.'

'I have to go back the day after tomorrow. The fools can't get on with the war without me.'

'Oh.'

Oh!

'Miss de Vraie wanted at the desk!'

'Excuse me.'

The boots looked up at Julie under his chocolate-box hat.

'Here you are, miss!'

'Thanks very much.'

She gave him a penny. The boots looked at the coin, spun it and put it in his pocket.

Julie lit the Kerry Blue. It crackled and burnt right up to the end.

The last straw!


'I hate hysterical girls. All my life I've avoided histrionics. Please be quiet.'

There was an accordionist playing to a group of people on the platform of Westland Row Station. An old man bent down and put a pound of butter in his socks: 'Don't forget to drink something out of the bottle before you go through the Customs.'

'Who are you telling?'

There's the train!

'You've been asked to get out of the way.'

And maybe someday I'll come back to Ireland
If it's only at the closing of my day . . .

'Goodbye, Nicholas.'

And see again the moon rise over Claddagh
And watch the sun go down on . . .

'Look after yourself!'

# PART V

# 23

The dew was evaporating already as I galloped the mare round the meadow beyond the lawn in front of the house. Girvan Castle, with its original keep, hidden by the vast Georgian structure, slept like a grey beast in the dawn. The mare's sides heaved as I bent to unlatch the gate; she'd lost condition during my absence.

'Well, you're back,' Lord Girvan stated.

'Yes, Lord Girvan.'

The lord, dressed for parade drill, surveyed his 'stable'. Three horses and three ponies. He clicked his heels as another would grind his teeth.

I was out of sympathy now with all of Girvan. The summer had blazed away and dried up every root and mortal. I just wanted to see Bernard as soon as possible so as I could forget Dublin, forget my hopes that had been raised and then dropped, forget Nicholas and his suave heartlessness. What had he done for me except buy me drinks? He'd given me the odd kiss to keep me quiet.

'Miss de Vraie.'

'Yes, Lord Girvan.'

'We'll be going over to Ballycullen this morning to mend a wind-charger belonging to some friends.'

'Yes, Lord Girvan.'

What is reality, anyway? I asked myself as I groomed the horses. Is it your mother telling you not to speak with your mouth full? Or is it chasing up and down Dawson Street, Dublin? Or is it standing up to your waist in mud and allowing Germans to shoot at you? Or the British? Or is it standing knee-high in clean straw tickling the undersides of horses?

'We'll leave about eleven.'

'Yes, Lord Girvan.'

Some hours later we were trotting up a long avenue lined with sycamore, oak, chestnut and rhododendron . . .

Here one had to forgive. They had planted these marvellous trees, built these beautiful houses. In the mosaic of the sun and shade, I walked my horse as far behind Lord Girvan's as possible.

The house was different from the average. It had been built in two styles. The hall door was on the extreme left; it leaned down over tall curving steps, with bulging bow windows to the right. A lady who stood at the top of the steps came down and greeted the lord. Lord Girvan didn't introduce us but she circumnavigated the horse's heels and came up to me, holding out her hand.

'I'm Leonie Nestor. Do come in. We'll stable the horses.'

I dismounted and shook hands: 'Julie de Vraie. I'm helping to look after the showjumpers and the children,' I said vaguely.

The lord too dismounted with a 'humph' and, taking his horse, I led the two of them into the yard, with Miss Nestor, taking short quick steps, leading the way.

She was tall and thin as a tulip, like Emily – tougher, of course, but as charming. She had a sister, as tall as she, but without her transparency of skin; a transparency which seems to evoke centuries of families shut away in remote Brontë-esque situations, that in each generation produce one who, because of reserve and sensitivity, is unable to take part wholeheartedly in the boisterous family-worship shared by their kin.

The other sister was, in comparison, run-of-the-mill, weather-beaten, masculine, but hospitable too.

It was nice to be welcomed in front of the lord, who harrumphed and went off to the yard in high dudgeon. It was dreadful for him to have his servant treated as a 'lady'.

In spite, however, of the ladies' wishing to spoil me with cakes and kindness, the afternoon dragged. It was just a question of passing the time till evening, when I'd see Bernard, with visions of my Dublin trip, which had contributed nothing to my pride. The last day had been the worst. Nicholas had bought me a present, like a nail for my coffin. He had been cold all day; he'd stayed, reluctantly, at Una's, rising at the crack to catch the boat. He had been uncomfortable with Una and Dennis and they had been most understanding. And then at Westland Row. Ugh! I couldn't bear to think about it.

Miss Leonie Nestor came out to see us off.

'Do come again,' she said. 'The afternoon was delightful.'

I murmured politely but there was a darkness on me. I knew I wouldn't. We trotted down the avenue, the lord, extremely bothered, leading the way.

# 24

'Dar . . . ling!'

'Bernard.'

We'd met on the avenue.

'My God! You're thinner than ever! Holding you is like being on my own!'

'Why are we standing here? Can't we go inside? Is Gerry there?'

'Not Gerry!'

'Oh God!'

Suddenly I knew.

With a married man!

Somewhere in the dark, in the past before I left for Dublin, I'd heard them say it and I'd paid no attention. Thinking they spoke of something else.

'Your wife?'

'No. Don't be difficult. And where the hell have you been?'

'But there's somebody?'

'Yes.'

'God, Bernard, why didn't you tell me?'

'Because it makes no difference to us.'

'Not to you because you knew all the time. Am I supposed to take it lying down?'

'Yes. And with me.'

'I can't. What's her name, anyway?'

'Rose.'

Rose!

'You're not married?'

'Not to her.'

'Christ. Who else is mixed up in all this? You have a wife as well?'

'Had. She became a tiger mother when her children were born. Wouldn't let me near her. Or the kids. It fizzled out. She's in America. Now you know it all. All my dark and venal past. In one sentence. Julie . . . you're crying.'

'I'm sorry!'

When I was small, my sister enjoyed putting a pillow over my head. The terror of dying! The inability to scream! It was like that now. A similar, but predictable, claustrophobia.

Suddenly we were sitting under a yew tree. The dog was there.

'He'll bark if he hears steps,' Bernard said.

'When did it all begin?'

'Quite some time back. Rose's husband was over in Dublin getting Celtic designs for his carpets.'

'And you met in Davy Byrnes?'

'Something like that. He had my name as a sort of intelligent artistic layabout and he thought that he might incorporate my skills with his money.'

'So you stole his wife?'

'Yes. There was all sorts of tedium about guns and fisticuffs.'

'So you unarmed him and disarmed Rose.'

'Very witty! As a matter of fact I was going to tell you about it when you disappeared. And so. Where were *you*?'

'Well . . . Wasn't it convenient?'

'No!' I thought he was going to clout me.

'Well, I was in Dublin!' I snapped.

I pulled a piece of grass out of its socket and chewed the tender yellow stalk.

'I'd better go, so.'

There was silence. The bull terrier scratched for fleas.

'Perhaps you should meet her now. Get it over with.'

I stared ahead, chewing.

'Don't worry,' he said. 'Rose is a decent old stick!'

Rose, fair and golden and poised, had already altered the personality of Bernard's home. I shouldn't have gone up with him. I should have allowed myself time to think. Consequently my awkward childishness became exaggerated; I left as quickly as possible.

'Come again,' she said, in a sing-song flyaway manner.


'I don't want to hurt you.'

We had met by arrangement, the following evening. He had picked me up at the cross and we were into the country away from Girvan. I ducked into the passenger seat below window level as we passed the castle gates.

'Nobody wants to hurt anybody. It's the way it is . . . '

'Some people do. Especially women.'

'They have more to lose.'

'So you went to Dublin. Without telling me. Did you go to see that Nicholas?'

'Yes. And no. I thought he might, I might . . . find a method of escape.'

'And it didn't work.' Bernard was very warm, very gentle.

'So he's gone back.'

'Poor lamb.'

He stopped the car in a laneway.

'Now. Come here.'

'It's all over,' I said.

He kissed me. 'Do you still think so?' He kissed me again: 'Well?'

'And what if she finds out?'

'Rose is quite cognisant of the male ego.'

'Even so!' I foresaw dreadful scenes.

'Damn this steering wheel,' he said. 'Let's get out.'

'No.'

No. No. No.

He sat back. He removed his arm from my shoulder and placed his hand on the steering wheel, looking sideways at me.

'No?'

He started the car and backed out on the road.

After a disastrous silence, I said: 'I'm sorry.'

'Shall I drop you off at your gate?'

'God, no!'

'You can come to supper, I suppose. But we'll have to be careful.'

'I thought you said Rose . . . '

'Oh, shut up! There's what's known as circumspection.'

'God, don't be so sarcastic,' I said, confused by his varying temper. He shrugged, unmoved, or pretending to be.

Rose swished her straight blonde hair at Bernard as we went in.

'I bumped into Julie,' he said.

Rose said laconically: 'I've a mess of curried beans and rice which you can share. Bernard has made this place into an inartistic pigsty and I'm trying to straighten it out.'

'I've had tea.'

'How very bourgeois.' Rose unconsciously echoed Bernard's criticism of me the first day we'd met.

It was a wretched moment.

'I work for an unsympathetic earl and I can't help the way I'm fed.'

Rose smiled.

'Gerry!' she shouted.

'At your service, ma'am!' Gerry stopped, seeing me, came forward: 'Hello,' he said awkwardly, not wanting to endanger Bernard by presuming he knew me too well. I wished I hadn't come.

'Have we any whiskey?' Rose said.

Gerry fetched the bottle and Rose poured us all out a glass.

'Here's cheers,' she said, as if the atmosphere was all sweetness and love.

The whiskey went down fast. Between each measure, my glass got warm in my hand.

'Children nowadays drink a lot,' Rose said. 'Your generation will have shorter lives.'

I tried to penetrate her mind. Did she suspect? Or was she always like this: on guard.

But the whiskey, perhaps, made her warm a little towards me.

The demon inside me wanted us to be friends. I tried to act as if Bernard and I had been acquaintances, merely, for that's how it had to be in future.

'I'd better be going,' I said. Bernard got up. Rose said: 'Anytime.' Bernard sat down. I didn't look at him.

I let myself out. I walked slowly down the avenue. Sometimes I stopped and stood staring into the black darkness of the yew trees. If a bird ruffled its feathers, or a leaf dropped, the noise roused me to continue my journey. Then, suddenly, I recalled I had no bike. I went back to the house, knocked, and Gerry let me in.

'Do you think Bernard could drive me home? I've no bike.'

'Shh,' Gerry said. 'They've just had an awful row. She's gone to bed. Wait down the avenue. I'll tell him.'

I darted off, running all the way to the road. In a moment or two, the headlights arced over the trees. He leant over and opened the door.

He drove a few hundred yards and then stopped. He pulled me over.

'I won't come round any more. It's too uncomfortable.'

'She's a bitch. But she'll soon change her tune.' He snatched the rug out of the back of the car and dragged me into a field. We went a little way till he found a hidden spot.

A strange ambience, developed between Rose and me, irked Bernard.

'Attraction of opposites isn't in it,' he once said.

148

And yet her suave resplendence when she sat still like an old icon was my fascination; I would stare at her, receding into Neanderthal bewilderment in my effort to learn.

She said: 'I'll have to have the bastard in Dublin. I wouldn't trust any of those Girvan quacks.'

So that was it!

I saw the loose dress and the curve on her stomach for the first time; I did not envy her.

But afterwards I felt more lonely.

# 25

In the castle, things went on as before. Like Canute holding back the sea, I tried to hold back the waves of disapproval transmitted from the Hon. Mrs Hermione Travers. Rose, perhaps, had put a new interpretation on things for me but my own paranoia kept its unique complexities going by keen observation; the group hatred was not imaginary.

Lazily, however, I rode the bridle path. When not schooling the mare for the show, I took the little girl on a leading rein and we trotted through the woods. The summer at Girvan might have petered out, the apples fallen, the rhododendron flower been trampled, and I might have departed with the swallows at the appointed hour. But, as these birds swoop and skim to warn you of approaching storms, so the demon inside me was working away. The desire to excel, to prove, even to my enemies, that I wished to please them, made me make a wrong decision.

I had inspired a good deal of confidence in the little girl and I thought it time she was let off the rein. I suggested this to her in the woods, where the sluggish pony was least likely to make off. She looked nervous, and if I'd had a tittle of wit, I wouldn't have insisted. For a while we proceeded side by side. I asked how she felt. She didn't reply. I bent over to catch her pony's rein but the animal, sensing my urgency, shook its head and bounded forward, sliding away from my grip. I was in a quandary; if I outdistanced the pony on my horse, the child would probably fall off, as the pony would be sure to gather speed. If I stopped, the child would think I wasn't trying to help her. But I had to stop; it was the lesser of the two evils.

'Try to pull on its mouth,' I kept shouting.

But the child had lost all control; the reins dangled uselessly as she hung on to the pony's mane. Then the pony swerved, and off she came. She was screaming with terror. I tried to muffle her yells by pressing her face against my body; I felt sorry for her but much more sorry for myself. The small tortured creature did not want to be a 'big strong girl', never in fact 'ever wanted to ride', and when I got her back to the castle, she fled inside like a rabbit with a wolf after it.

I went in to lunch.

I came out again.

Nothing happened.

No one appeared to pull me off the horse, to sack me, to shoot me.

I cursed my foolhardiness, my misjudgement. Ironically, had she been badly hurt, their genuine feelings would have crowded out their desire to attack me. There was nothing for it but to wait.

And sure enough, that evening while I was ironing a shirt in the annexe of the kitchen, mother and daughter entered in full sail. I got the waft of Desdemona's perfume at the door; musk for mystery!

There was no preamble: 'That was a silly thing to do!'

Say something! Are you dumb?

Mrs Travers was churning herself up into a nervous hysteria. No sex life; bad for the metabolism.

I burned myself on the flat iron and cried out.

'Ha,' said Desdemona, as if this was another sin.

'You realise what you did this afternoon and what it means.' Lady Girvan had now entered into the attack.

'I'm sorry, Lady Girvan. Very sorry,' I managed to say.

She went on to say that my reprehensible behaviour was becoming the talk of the county; that 'woodcutter' was referred to like Hitler, the common enemy of mankind, and then back to the afternoon's incident: 'We did at least think we could trust you with the children.'

'If we let you stay on, it will only be because of the show; there's some doubt that O'Hagan will be free then after all.'

You old bitch, I thought, you'd been planning all the time for O'Hagan to have my rides.

'If my daughter had been hurt, you, you, would have been responsible. Do you realise this? Or are you so steeped in your own selfish pursuit of pleasure that you wouldn't care? I wouldn't be at all surprised. People like you are responsible for wars, through your stupidity, selfishness and greed.'

Mother of God!

'I am sorry,' I said again, feebly.

'Not much good being sorry, now!' said Desdemona.

Then suddenly I exploded: 'Shut up . . . shut up . . . will you . . . I made a mistake. I genuinely thought your daughter was ready to ride alone. I'm sorry. I can't say any more.'

'You have no manners,' Desdemona screamed.

I picked up the flat iron.

'Oh dear,' Lady Girvan said.

I ran from the room, up the stairs two at a time, into my room, and leaned against the door. I still held the flat iron, which I hadn't thrown. I shook from head to toe. I could have murdered her; it was quite plain. I could have murdered her. What was I to do? Where was I to go? I lay on my bed face down, my hands clenched on the sheets, without making a sound. I expected that they would change their minds and fire me in the morning. Gradually I withdrew behind the bars of madness.

# 26

I pedalled along; I counted the potholes in the road, the gaps in the hedges, the shores, the tufts of grass, the spots where the camber was steep where the wheel might skid and my knees could get scored if I didn't look out. I counted the cottages, as square as hen houses, all housing Girvan estate workers, some friendly, but most of them afraid of the almighty and all-seeing eye of Lord Girvan, an eye that would poke into the soul and gouge out the rottenness with carrion accuracy. They were dead, these people; the young ones only getting the bit of football on Sundays after churchgoing had been exploited to the limits of its usefulness; after they'd been seen in line and counted. I pedalled beyond the straight hill that rears from the Girvan Castle gates till I reached the posts with the two lions, the ear chipped off one of them by wind and time, the stone scarred by surface lichen. The old bike wouldn't take the rutted avenue; the front wheel twisted from side to side. I threw the bike into the nettles and felt my way along in the dead dark with my whispering feet. And soon I reached the house with the drawing-room windows on a line with the front door, curtainless and bright to the evening sky. The boxed-up front door defied my entering and, peering through the window, I saw the broken table had keeled over towards the wall.

I walked through the long grass that stretched right up to the windows till I was in a miasma of muddy ruts, cart-tracks and cattle-hoof marks; my shoes squelched, stuck in the mud; I took them off and, barefoot, pressed on through the filth, the cow-shit squirting through my toes; I found what I was looking for: the open door. The outer scullery door had never properly closed, and I stood now on the cold stone flags, for the moment unsure, then I walked straight into the front hall and turned right into the drawing room and, going to Emily's desk, began scattering through her notes, pulling out old lists and catalogues; I was searching for something. At that moment, I was not quite sure what it was, but I had to find it. I found nothing; I paced up and down the worn carpet and, precisely as she must have, I retraced my steps to the back of the house and, still barefoot, felt my way along the passage that led to the greenhouse.

Holding the powdery walls away from my face, I went step by step, each one more agonisingly uncertain than the last, until a faint light suddenly showed up shards of glass where the door had been broken down on a hot summer's afternoon; la de dah, she had put the key in her pocket after locking the door behind her! A moon, that must be somewhere, caused a sinister glow, and I could see the dancing plants, her passion; here the agile lady must have waited till all was still and climbed up the ladder, for such is life!

There was a sudden sound; a rustle, a fumbling. A bird? A rat? A bat? I whirled around and around, searching the dimness, but there was nothing. I searched the ceiling and the beams that criss-crossed, shadowing the glass panes, and then I saw it! The pale hemp rope with the careful reef knot and the double ends of the lasso that had been hacked through. Now as then! I saw the neck jerk suddenly and the silly shoes tumble slowly off the thin pointed feet. Emily!

The ladder lay parallel to the low wall shelving the flowerbeds and I knew how simple it would be to jerk it onto its feet and run up it; a graceful gesture on a crazy trapeze.


My bicycle lay as I had left it; it was farcically easy to lift it out of the undergrowth, and even though it shook like I did, I felt an insane thrill as my hands clasped the chrome-plated handlebars; if God exists, he is surely two wheels and a rickety frame; my only friend! And Emily? Well, she lies in the graveyard over the hill.

154

# 27

The next day came and went; I dully went about my duties; they hadn't changed their mind, but no one came near the yard; none of the family wanted a ride. I didn't school the mare in case she would get stale; I took her for a long walk on the roads, my mind blank; I went deep into the country. When it was still broad daylight, I cycled briskly to Bernard's house.

I approached quietly; it had become a habit; I was ready for a tonal warning not to proceed; if voices were raised, I always beat a retreat. I had been right to go easy. Voices were raised.

'Go and fuck her then, the little slut. Talk about Indian summer; you're in the dotage . . . she has no *chic* . . . no *élan*, just a mess. And she's mad about you . . . why don't you marry her?'

'You know I'm not free to marry anyone. If Simone divorced me, I'd probably marry you.'

She would have a name like Simone, I thought irrelevantly.

'If it wasn't her, it'd be someone else,' Rose continued. 'You don't give a damn about her. It's just the virgin image, the little girl lost. You're a megalomaniac, you simply can't do without constant flattery,' and then like in a comic, something heavy went flying: *wham*! And *wham* again. Obviously the wall took the missile because there were no groans.

I crept away. No need to hear any more.

Rows and reconciliations.

I don't think they fought like that very often. Once on the road, I got off my bike and sat down in the grass. If Bernard takes the male prerogative, he'll storm out. He'll come to me, hold out his hand, and together we will walk into oblivion; no more return.

At eleven o'clock, stiff, I rose. I wiped the dew off the handle-bars with the sleeve of my shirt and I steered myself home.

Home.

What's it like to live in a castle? I'll tell you. There is a room where nobody goes. It's called the library. There are many books; brown bound volumes line the walls. In one corner there is an upright Blüthner, on which stands a splayed candelabra made of embossed silver. There are four candles. They are never lit.

I sat down at the piano and played Bach's fourth two-part invention. I knew it off by heart.

Rose and Bernard will be asleep by now.

Am I not just a right stupid whore of an idiot?

'What are you doing at this hour of the night, keeping the whole house awake?'

'Playing the piano.'

'This is now the limit. It's a disgusting noise.' The figure held the candlestick aloft. 'I'll have to tell Lord Girvan about this. I only hope my mother hasn't been woken up. After the strain of the day, she needs what rest she can get.'

I'm sure you care.

I closed the lid of the piano. I got up and walked past her.

'The piano needs tuning,' I said. 'It shouldn't be allowed to get so damp. If I were you, I'd have the fire lit here from time to time.'

I thought she would pound me on the head with her candle-stick, but I ducked and sped up the stairs. I turned the key in the mortice lock. Safe again . . .

# 28

Mooney buys the drinks and I demolish them.

'That fellow with the two-tone Ford? I believe he has a class of a wife now?'

'That's right . . . '

'Wouldn't want to disagree with her.'

'She's quite nice.'

'Hard as nails.'

'That's only the impression she gives.'

'I'd say she was a few months gone.'

'What do you think of him?'

'He's all right. A bit Englishy. They buy stuff from me . . . plaster . . . cement.'

'Can I have another brandy?'

'You'd need an oil well in the Middle East to keep you in drinks.'

'Sorry.'

'I don't care how much you drink. Are you back again? Have you finished with him? I've missed you awfully. I'd buy you the Pacific Ocean if you asked. Provided they'd take a cheque. Do you know what, you're the nicest person I've ever met. Remember what I used to call you? My magazine-cover girlie . . . '

'In any case, Des, how did you know that I was interested in Bernard and his wife?'

'Do you think I go around with dark glasses on?'

'I'm sorry,' I said again.

'Saint Desmond, that's me.' He paused a minute and then covered my hand with his. 'You see, I love you. That's why.'

I looked into his massive dark face and large brown eyes; his cheeks were puffy with the approach of middle age; his suit, which he wore for work and play, was shiny at the seams; it needed renewing from Burton's the Tailor of Taste.

'Come down to the shop after and I'll get the hackney to drive you home.'

'I can't . . . oh of course I will.'

Out of the dimming of my drunken faculties, I recalled once in the beginning of our friendship how he had swung me onto the counter of his shop; he had run his hand up my skirt – I'd let it rest there for just long enough – then quite gently he put his finger on my clitoris; I'd jumped down – made a joke – said hurriedly: 'Lets go for a drink.' He was still staring at me.

'Strictly speaking, I ought to shave three times a day,' Bernard often said after he'd scored my face into a map of painful weals. Why shouldn't I let Des throw me down among the iron filings, burst cement bags, in the dark recesses of his shop; under the shadow of the axe-head, in a bed of netting wire? Why why why?

I lurched away from the bar, tottering towards the stairs . . . An old English sheepdog was outside the lavatory. If I were Rose, I'd say: 'Animals are a bore.' I laughed and said: 'Animals are a bore . . . ha ha . . . Animals are a bore . . . ha ha ha.'

I slopped my next brandy all over the bar and laughed and laughed. 'Desy, darling, can I drive the car home? We'll put the bleeding bike in the boot . . . do you like my alliteration, bleeding bike in the — '

'Shh.'

'What's up? You know I'm an excellent driver . . . I was first in last year's Grand Prix.'

'There's a war on and there happens to have been no Grand Prix.'

'A grand pricks,' I said.

'And there'll be a war here quite soon.'

I was obviously getting very tiresome. But I was too drunk to care.

'Lovely war. The Germans dropping bombs like pimples all over England, doing vice versa to Germany. The world is mad . . . mad . . . *mad* . . . *mad*.'

I fell off the bar stool and had to be dragged to my feet.

'That was very funny. Did I ever tell you about the Czech I met in Dublin? I don't mean the bouncing Czech either . . . well, she would have said "Ferry vunny". Ferry vunny . . . ha ha . . . Isn't that vunny?'

'You'll have us both thrown out.'

'I can't serve the lady any more drinks,' the barman said.

'He says,' I said, pointing my finger at the barman, 'th'ould cod, that I'm drunk. He infers I'm drunk . . . th'ould begrudging cod.'


On the third morning, I couldn't get up. I had alcoholic poisoning.

Please God, I prayed, let me die. I was doubled up with cramps in the stomach. I retched until I felt I was as empty as a trussed hen. The lord himself came to my bedside. He didn't stay long. Nellie had cleared away the bucket and opened the window but the sweet sickly smell was unmistakable; you'd need to be a Pioneer not to recognise it. The doctor came and, with a sly look, diagnosed 'grumbling appendix'. In the way of all country doctors, he drove a little black car with a little petrol mixed with paraffin in the tank. He was a joke . . . good . . . I was a joke . . . bad. He snapped his bag shut and gave me a bottle: 'That'll settle your tum.'

Late that evening, I tottered out of bed. I made up my face like a Woolworth's tart. I did a little jig to experiment with my stomach pains. I thought about Cairns ale. The *aqua vitae* could wait.

Come doon the back stairs when you come to court me,
Come as ye came and let naebody see.

I was on the road again, free. Past Mrs Brennen's cottage. What do you see, Mrs Tow-eyed Brennen? You see a girl on a bicycle hurrying to her secret tryst under the yew trees.

A two-tone Ford was rumbling into view. Without caring, I threw the bike into the ditch and climbed in beside him.

'I've been every evening to the corner looking for you.'

'You can't expect me to live three whole days without you.'

'I'm sorry, Bernard, I've been on the booze.' I always seemed to be apologising for something.

'Has that effing airman been back?'

'How did you know he was an airman? Besides, he's never been in an aeroplane. He's an intelligence something.'

'Do you think I care?'

'And no, I haven't been further than Girvan.'

'I can't see what you want with that ridiculous ironmonger.'

'I don't want anything. That's the whole point.'

'So you arse around with him in preference to being with me.'

'But Rose, she's like Cerberus.'

'Rose, me arse.'

'Please, Bernard, don't be cross. I'm very sick.' And as if to prove this, I rolled down the window.

'You ought to carry a paper bag around with you.'

'Where can we go that's warm? I don't want you in the dew.'

'There's the anti-vampire wood. With acres of pine needles.'

'Lead me to it.'

We turned off the road. The car stalled in the cart-track ruts.

'That's my last spring gone. Get out.' He leant over me and opened the door and shoved me into the nettles. I thought he was going to try and back out, so I lay there feeling the blisters rise on my bare legs.

'It's cosy here,' I said.

But he got out on his side and, with the bull terrier's blanket under his arm, plunged through the growth. 'Fucking nettles,' he said. 'Come on.'

I ran after him just as I'd cycled after the bishop's son that hot morning the century before last. I took off the high-heeled shoes that I wore for the benefit of the Girvan gentry and plunged barefoot over the ruts; the hard earth, like the pebbles on Killiney beach, bruised the instep.

'My feet are in flitters,' I yelled.

'Cut them off,' he yelled back.

'Smells like a French restaurant.'

'That's the garlic.'

'I'll say.'

'Don't make me feel small.'

'You are small . . . that's why I love you.'

'You sound as if you were trying to convince yourself.'

'I don't *want* to love you . . . it's the last thing I want.'

'Bernard, why are you in such a temper?'

'Do you let that puffy peasant fuck you?'

'I don't know.'

'What do you mean, you don't know. If you do, I'll kill you . . . '

He put his two hands on my throat and began to squeeze. I could not squeak . . . breathe . . . he wouldn't, couldn't do it . . . could he?

He let go.

'But you're in bed with Rose every night.'

'That's not the point.'

'But you took her from her husband.'

'Yes I did, and I wanted to. And from her child. I took a mother from her baby . . . how does that shock your petty bourgeois mind? Suburbia. Ironmongery.'

'Oh lay off, Bernard, give me a break.'

There was a long cold silence.

'I thought you were different,' he said at last, 'but it turns out you're just like the rest, stupid, inconsistent, unreliable, opinionated.'

161

'I'd better go, it's not fair. I've had enough. I never voice my opinions.'

'No, but you act on them. Do you think it's fair to me?' he shouted.

'But you're much older than me; you know how it is. I've learnt a lot from you as it is.'

'You don't seem to remember it.'

'And anyway, I didn't with Mooney.'

'You're sure? Say you're sure. Are you certain, baby?' He leant over and unbuttoned my shirt. 'You're so thin, darling, but you have the most beautiful shoulders I've ever seen. Apart from your feet, they're the sexiest thing about you.'

'The sexiest thing about you is your eyes. Pop-eyes.'

'Hyper-thyroid.' He pulled my skirt down my legs until I lay naked on the dog blanket. He caressed me with his hands and gradually put his head between my legs.

'What's that?' He jumped away; he threw the dog blanket round me; I doubled myself up.

'It's gone.'

'Man or woman?'

'Don't know.'

'Did he see us?'

'Don't know. But you may be sure he did.'

'Oh Jesus, it'll be all over the country, communicated from bush to bush, from tree to tree.' I got up and dressed. 'Oh Jesus, that's all I need.'

'It doesn't matter.'

'It may not matter to you but it affects me. This is what they've been waiting for. The other day, the child fell off and got frightened. It was my fault and they showered me with blame. This is their prayers answered.'

'Oh, what does it matter if you have to leave. You're so bloody paranoid.'

'There's a lot of difference between being paranoid and being a victim of jealousy and morality.'

'They're a lousy shower to work for, anyway.'

'That's not the point. One nearly always dislikes one's employer. Some are worse than others, and these are pretty bad. But it's the only job I've got. And I have to prove I can keep it. And it's near you.'

'That affects you?'

'It does.'

Another silence. Not as bad as the first.

'Well. I'd come to see you every week in Dublin.'

'Every week? I thought you couldn't live three days without me.'

'If I see you every week, I see you every week. If I see you every day, I see you every day. Are you cold?'

'You'd learn to get on without me. Yes, I'm freezing.'

He kissed me; his face was cold.

'Did you see who it was?'

'A complete stranger.'

'You're trying to cheer me up. There's no such thing.'

'There must be some. From the other side of the county?'

'Not Brennen?' I persisted.

'How could he get here?'

'One of his cohorts could have seen me get into the car and followed us here. His eldest son probably saw the car pass the castle. Anything at all. Pure coincidence.'

'Never mind, baby. See what happens.'

He took me by the hand and we walked towards the car. We had to push it out of the ruts and then he slowly backed out while I walked beside, directing him. Eventually we hit the tarmac and I got in. Bernard got in too, but didn't start the car.

'All that bloody nonsense,' he said, 'was because we haven't been together for so long. I'm a frustrated old man.'

'Is sex the only thing that matters to you?'

'I thought it was, but apparently not. I get other ideas as well.'

'You mean about work, ambition, the future?'

'No, about you.'

There was more silence. I didn't know what to think. Except that he couldn't leave Rose.

'When's the child due?'

'September, October.'

'And she'll have it in Dublin?' I was saying anything to get away from the main issue. 'Are you interested in it? Its sex or anything?'

'What an idiotic question. I don't even want a pet mouse, let alone another baby. Go through all that again . . . '

Another silence . . . and still he didn't start the car.

'I've no desire to procreate, and never had. It's a bad seed. Even the most intelligent women think they can trap you with an infant; they never learn . . . but it's only another nail in the coffin. Men just can't indulge in the fatherhood bit . . . not in the same soak-it-in way women do.'

'You mean men are never even proud of their children? That's ridiculous . . . '

'Oh, some men . . . All right . . . You should have never met me . . . I'm a monster . . . go on, say it . . . ' Bernard was smiling. 'And mark you, it's harder to shed a mistress than a wife. Women choose their husbands. Men choose their mistresses . . . mostly . . . ' He was giving no quarter . . . wasn't in fact going to be trapped into saying anything.

'What keeps people together, then? I mean, millions of people stick it out . . . till death etc . . . '

'Or debt . . . '

'You might end up marrying Rose . . . '

Bernard turned on me. 'What do you mean?' having no idea that I'd sneaked up on one of their rows. 'Once bitten . . . '

'No . . . no,' I said.

'What is it? What do you want, Julie?'

'Good heavens, me? I want to be left with a few personal beliefs, that's all . . . '

Bernard got extremely kind.

'You musn't believe anything . . . anything at all . . . What you *feel* is quite different.' He put his arms round me, awkwardly, in the car. 'Oh what a fuck-up,' he said. 'We're back in this damn car again.'

'And what *I* feel is also quite different.'

He switched on the ignition and we drove slowly home; we passed the castle gates and on to the other side of Brennen's cottage.

He pulled in to the side.

The bicycle, a heap of twisted iron, was lying in the ditch. Tied with a lump of string to the handlebars was a piece of paper.

Wearily I got out. Wearily I humped the machine on to the road. I unscrewed the piece of paper. Scrawled on the back of an invoice headed 'Earl of Girvan Estates Ltd', in crooked printing was: 'HAVE A GOOD LICK'.

I held it for a long time; I turned to go. Bernard was watching me. I simply nodded and got on the bike.

'Julie.'

'Goodbye,' I said.

## 29

The engine went. Paraffin had put paid to it.

We walked in the rain. It eased off a bit. Cold showers interspersed with watery sunshine. We were at his gate; I had been visiting them, drinking Rose's whiskey. I was a bit jarred and Bernard had made an excuse to see me to the road.

He pulled me into the little corrugated iron-roofed shed that was part of the new building for the intended factory.

'Not here! Rose might follow us down if you're missing too long.'

'We're sheltering.'

The rain had begun in earnest.

He pushed me against the timber wall.

'I can't stand it much longer,' he said.

'Stand what?'

'Rose's bitching. But also your attitude. Vague.'

'Vague?' I said. 'Vague? What can I do? Either I come to the house or I don't see you at all.'

'And we haven't been together for ages. Alone. We might as well take up bridge.'

'Why is Rose bitching you? Me?'

'Oh, you . . . money . . . pregnancy . . . tiredness . . . Pregnant women are awful. Like sado-masochistic cows.'

'Christ, Bernard, she can't be that bad.'

The timber hard against my back, Bernard, hard, pressing me against the timber.

'Right,' he said. 'We'll go away this weekend.'

'I can't. You know I can't.'

The rain beat on the iron roof with relentless fury.

'And why not?'

'Because of the show,' he mimicked.

'And Rose.'

'And what have those two items to do with us?'

'I have to school the mare again. She hasn't been out for days. And the show's on Wednesday. And Rose's child is due in a month; you can't leave her.'

'I happen to love her, the stupid old bitch; but at the moment, I just can't stand her. So you're coming to town with me on Saturday.'

'I'm not. I'd love to, but I can't.'

'"I'd love to. Come to the ball with me. A cocktail party. Oh, darling, I've nothing to wear." That's what you sound like.'

'And so you love Rose?'

'That's right. Now start crying. Maa . . . maa . . . '

'Let me go, you bastard.'

'Julie, Christ, I'm sorry. It's not easy for me either.'

He caressed me, stroked my face. I was exhausted from his constant change of mood.

'I love you,' I said meekly.

'You do in my arse. You love your stupid self.'

'There you go again.'

'Love is a tedious overworked habit-forming occupation. Let's not entangle ourselves with it.'

But he held me with the arms swathed tightly round me as if he knew that I must escape soon or never. And he kissed me many times till the hands worked downwards and pulled up the cotton frock.


*'Whoring.'*

The voice was harsh. That's the way it had to be.

'How dare you spy on me?'

'You're in your second childhood,' Rose said bitterly.

Rose turned her back. Turned her back on the two defenceless bodies who had leapt apart when she shouted. I started for the door.

Rose said: 'There's no point in your going now.'

I stood. Rose laughed. A little acid laugh that ran away into nothing. Like the rain.

'Get back to the house,' Bernard said.

'Get back to the house,' Rose mimicked.

And the three of us stood together alone. Each had a separate problem; each of us seeming to suffer the most. We could try to understand each other's feelings but we couldn't change identities.

And if I was only myself, Julie de Vraie, I was also an anonymous quantity coming between Rose and Bernard; a quantity just as great or small as Rose chose to make it, and only she could decide how to acquit herself in this situation.

But Bernard was angry. His rage flared up into terrifying strength; it was remote and personal and scarcely involved either of us. His masculine freedom had been threatened; he would maintain it; he would stay with either or both or neither of us, just as he chose; would be answerable for no action. He exchanged supercilious stare with supercilious stare. He brushed past Rose, leaving me without a word; without him, I hadn't a single weapon; I was defenceless and in the wrong.

'We'll let the old man cool off,' Rose surprisingly said, and I took my cue and walked out of the shed into the rain. Climbed on to my bike and cycled away. In the rain. In the wrong.

> Oh, Rose, thou art sick
> The invisible worm . . .
> Hath found out thy bed . . .

'Nellie's been taken to the Infirmary.' The cook, Mrs O'Hagan, sat as usual, peering into the *Independent*, which she held aslant the Aladdin.

'The Infirmary?'

'Where else?' The cook turned back to the *Independent.*

'Did she collapse or something?'

'Aye.'

'What doing?'

'Taking my lady's maid's tray upstairs.'

'The lesser shall wait on the lesser.'

'And,' continued Mrs O'Hagan, glancing at me over her glasses, 'your friend has arrived.'

My heart gave a great jerk. '*My* friend?' I shouted.

'Yes. He's in the drawing room talking to Mrs Travers.'

I looked dully at the cook. I had actually thought she meant Nicholas, but of course she meant O'Hagan, her relation, my enemy. I laughed in a crazy manner: 'Ho ha,' I said. 'How very nice.'

Then there was the dream; the usual dream. The mother in the coffin. The small glazed fists were shiny and transparent and were beating against the wood.

'Hello, hello!' O'Hagan's tan jacket matched his hair.

'Hello, hello,' I said.

'Have their various lords and ladyships been out this morning?'

'Not since the monsoon season.'

'I'll give the mare a turn around.'

'You'll keep her out of the mud,' I said curtly.

As he vaulted on to the mare, he rammed his crutch and I had to turn away my face; he would have read stories there, stories with unhappy endings.

And he brought the animal back with rings of foam around its flanks.

'What a way to bring her back,' I said.

My remark, however, was offset by the arrival of a radiant Desdemona. 'It was too exciting, the way Bella took the jumps,' she said.

'Bella and I are old friends,' O'Hagan said, casting a sly look in my direction.

'You are a judge of co-ordination between hand and horse.'

Hand and arse!


'I've come to see Nellie McMahon.'

A small woman shuffled up a long corridor that smelled of disinfected urine. We went up winding stone stairs, in and out and past closed doors; she was bad-tempered and overworked and wouldn't answer my questions.

She held a door for me at last and pointed to the far corner of a long ward. Nellie the dying number was surely there.

On either side of the ward were beds on which lay the other women, the fat ones with swollen faces and the thin ones with sharp ragged features, but all of them had the same vacant expression in their eyes. They had given up.

When Nellie saw me, her eyes changed; the pupils grew large and dark and, without smiling, she followed my progress down the ward.

'Nellie, do you feel awful?'

'It's all right.'

I could hardly hear her voice. I sat on the side of her bed and could think of nothing to say.

'O'Hagan came,' I said eventually.

And Nellie said: 'Don't fret.'

'I brought you some raspberries.'

Nellie turned her head and her expression didn't change. She said: 'Thank you.'

I had never spoken to Lady Girvan about Nellie's chances of being sent to Dublin and now it was too late. Even if Lady Girvan hadn't taken any notice of my plea, at least I'd have made it. And was that really all that mattered; what I did and what I didn't do? Did it all boil down to that? That I should be able to live with less guilt? Nellie cold in her grave like Emily, or Nellie lying here in these sweet hospital smells with small pools of sweat gathering between her thighs and under her armpits, was, then, all the one to me?

'Have they got in touch with your sister?' I remembered how Nellie had told me about her once and how I'd seen her in my mind as an unwieldy woman surrounded by pasty-faced kids.

I wandered out into the corridor and tried to find the nurse. But the same woman who had led me up the stairs was in an anteroom piling soiled linen into a sluice.

'Is there a nurse I could talk to?'

It seemed the ward nurse was off duty but I could see her the following evening at half past six.

Yes, I could see her then, the woman said, reluctantly.

Outside, the grass was wreathed in damp vapour. I wiped the saddle with my sleeve and pedalled away up the hill. Death was the only prescription for the people behind those walls, and in my inadequacy I sped through the silent land. I had nowhere to go: I couldn't go to Bernard's, nor could I face going to Girvan, and returning to the castle was doom. I stopped at the front gates and sat astride the bike with my foot on the grass verge. No car passed, no cart, no human. I cycled up the avenue and threw the bike into the shed and walked slowly into the back part of the house. There were sounds of jollification. I tried to tiptoe past the kitchen but I bumped into O'Hagan carrying a crate of stout.

'Julie!' he cried. 'Do join us.'

'No thanks. I've just ridden a long way.'

'There's riding and riding.'

I ran up the back stairs into my room. I went to the window. I sat on my bed. I got up and walked about the floor. I could think of nothing except Bernard and Rose. I was desperate. I ran out of the room and along the top corridor, which led to the front part of the house. As I went, the furnishings got plusher, the carpets deeper, and I clattered down the central staircase and knocked loudly on the door facing the hall. The stuffed gnu gazed glumly into eternity and bright noises came from the drawing room. A voice said: 'Come in!'

The family seemed to be having a hooley too, if of a slightly different order. Decanters flashed and glasses clinked. I went up to Lady Girvan and said: 'Might I speak to you for a moment?'

And Lady Girvan, with a face like the north wind, looked at Lord Girvan, and he came over to me and literally frogmarched me out of the room.

'You can't interrupt people when they're entertaining!'

> The mission bells told me
> That I musn't stray
> South of the border . . .

O'Hagan's voice led the group.


My feet clattered up the stone steps that led to Nellie's ward.

'Is the sister, or staff nurse, here?'

'No, she's below in the kitchens.'

I clattered down the main staircase again, following my sense of smell. Various drab menials went about unsavoury tasks; the sister, easily identified amongst this heterogeneous crew, was addressing a Polish refugee who was shielding her face with her arms.

The sister caught sight of me and advanced without subtlety. 'Who are you?'

'It's about Nellie McMahon, who was admitted two days ago. How is she?'

The sister swept out of the kitchen and up the stairs; I followed.

'Is there anything that could be done for her?'

'All patients get the same treatment here.'

'What chances are there for her recovery?'

It was not ethical to discuss patients' chances with casual friends.

'Has her next of kin been told? Her married sister?'

It was none of my business. Snub after snub.

'What about morphine?'

The sister stopped and looked uncomprehendingly at me; she went into a room and shut the door. I stood on the landing till a girl came out carrying a tray of sterile instruments.

'Please, miss!' I beseeched her. 'I must talk to the sister. Will you please tell her I've been sent by Lady Girvan!'

The mention of 'the quality' arrested the attention of the girl much more successfully than if I'd said I was a messenger from God.

'Stay there. I'll be back in a sec.'

She poked her head out of the room with a nod and I entered.

'Come in, dear,' said the sister with revolting volte-face. 'Why didn't you tell me you were sent by her ladyship?'

Afraid of my tell-tale face, I hurriedly said that Lady Girvan wanted to know if Nellie would benefit by being sent to Dublin. The sister said that her growth was advanced. Ray treatment might not be efficacious; very expensive. And on the other hand . . .

'What about an operation?' I cut in.

'Out of the question at this stage.'

'In other words?'

'Yes, in other words.'

'I see.' I looked out of the window; the fields swept away beyond the road. In the tawdriness of late summer, the whole country seemed malevolent.

'Will the doctor be round soon?'

'He's due.'

'Perhaps I could talk to him?'

A strategic error on my part.

'He'll tell you little more than I have,' she snapped. But obviously feeling she still had to answer to Lady Girvan, she said: 'We do what we can. She's in good hands here, you know.'

Maintaining protocol or fooling the public was all the one to her; the public seldom cared anyway; the sick and the old were got rid of; consciences were at rest.

'I'll go in and see her anyway,' I said.

Nellie formed a quiet smile when she saw me and whispered how pleased she was.

'I've been talking to the sister and you may be moved to Dublin. You'd get better there more quickly.'

'Aye.'

'Don't you believe me?' I said in the darkness of a terrible melancholy.

'No. They won't do it.'

'They will, if Lady Girvan insists.'

'Aye.'

There was silence.

Again I remembered I had to insist on some painkiller. Nellie's features were still; what she suffered she hid behind those strangely soft eyes. I searched again for the ward sister; when I found her, she had reassumed her belligerent bearing.

'I've just been on the phone to Lady Girvan.'

This was it, then.

'What did she say?'

'She said that you had no authority to act on her behalf. Good day.' She pressed a bell on her desk. The same girl came in. 'Take this to 42.'

'Nellie must have morphine,' I shouted.

'You are trying to teach us our business?'

'Yes I am,' I screamed again. 'I'm going to see the doctor. He'll listen to me.'

The sister got up and came towards me. I raised my arm like the woman in the kitchen.

'Get out!' she screamed. 'Get out, get out! Before I call the Guards.'

174

I lingered at the castle gates. Lingered at the turn to Bernard's house. I cycled on into Girvan and pulled up at Mooney's shop. I banged on the shutters. I cycled down Main Street, past the Majestic, cycled back, stopped at Sheehan's bar and went in.

There was an old man at the counter and no other customer.

'A bottle of Cairns, please.'

'Sorry.'

'Sorry?'

'Can't serve you, miss.'


I went out of the bar and got on the bike. I cycled slowly out of Girvan and on to the castle road. Night was falling. Grey dusky shadows loomed at gates; cattle lumbered in muddy gaps; the corncrake rasped out its repetitive message. A figure on a bicycle passed, said 'Goodnight', passed on its way, the two bicycles going in opposite directions, one with a small light dangling, the other with no light; both machines rattled noisily till distance divided them.

Behind Emily's derelict gate, little animals scuttled about on their nightly journeyings. The two prisons: the one surrounded by cold gentility, trees and winds, the other by hurrying brutality, bare boards, cracked porcelain sluices, crevices filled with Jeyes fluid, which lodged in them with a rainbow film. No difference, really.

# 30

It was the last Sunday before the show. Normally people sat about in their Sunday clothes, doing as little work as possible, except, of course, the servants, who organised the meals and played their various parts in the serving thereof.

Julie de Vraie usually took her time over her meals; she attended church, cycling off before she was engaged in conversation after the service, returning to the castle, taking book and rug and going as far from the house as possible. But today, with the broken weather, she made the excuse of the imminence of the show to ride Bella out and give her a turn over the jumps.

O'Hagan came down the paddock just as Julie was heading for the double gate; Julie caught sight of him as she was gathering the mare to take off. The mare cleared the first gate and then, misjudging the position of the second one, jumped straight into it, tripped, tangled her legs, and Julie flew off into the air like a boomerang, coming down on her side. She leapt up, still holding the reins, calming the animal who'd restored her balance, and began feeling her legs for damage. There were no bumps or bruises, and she trotted the animal up and down; no harm done.

O'Hagan was grinning. They met each other's gaze; said nothing.

Julie looked towards the castle windows, wondering if Desdemona had seen the incident.

'She's all right,' Julie calmly said.

'Are you hurt?' O'Hagan said.

Julie jumped casually on to the mare and cantered to the gate. A voice called out: 'I think that proves that O'Hagan had better ride Bella in all the events; you can ride one of the others.'

'Yes?' Julie looked round for O'Hagan; he'd disappeared. 'I'll tell him.' She smiled at Desdemona. 'Good idea,' she added.

Desdemona was glittering for some departure or other; all jewels and purple cloth.

O'Hagan arrived in the yard when Julie was drying the horse. She whistled like a boy.

He stood near Julie in the stable.

She said: 'Excuse me!'

'I wouldn't like to see any of your pretty bones broken!' he said.

Julie ducked under the mare's belly to get away from him, angrily threw the rug over the mare, hitting him with the strap.

'So sorry,' she said. 'If you *will* stand there . . . '

'What did Mrs Travers say to you?'

'She asked me was I hurt.'

Julie gave the animal a final pat, pulled the girth to see if it was too tight, passed O'Hagan, and went into the yard. The latter followed, controlled. She was carrying the tackle, trailing the saddle girth, and he picked it up. She increased her pace, threw the saddle on to the stand in the harness room, turned, and was caught by O'Hagan. They swung round and he forced her into a corner. Julie twisted and twisted her face to avoid the biting kisses and the saliva that trickled from his mouth; she crouched like an animal and freed herself to run out into the yard, and he, following, with heavy frustrated panting and groaning, while the great house, head and shoulders above them, with the entire Girvan family, was, no doubt, watching the circus.

Once inside, she ran up to her room and began frantically to change her clothes ready to get away – anywhere, anyhow – and when she had to return, she'd lock herself into her room, if necessary.

177

Julie reached Bernard's gate at a quarter to four. Other Sundays, spent on the lawn, with laughter and drinking from the bottles, the dog scratching and Rose lazily honing her wit, were other Sundays. Today she must loiter like a criminal in circles and shadows, hoping for a glimpse of Bernard or a message to him via Gerry.

She cycled up and down the road, idled to Brennen's cottage and back to the gateway; clouds threatened, low, heavy grey; will it rain? And then back to the castle at six to snatch her food and wolf it down.

Julie went back to Bernard's gate; waited till darkness and tiptoed up where Rose's flat blonde hair described a concave arc, the flat face and high cheekbones in half-profile. He said: 'I'm going for a walk!'

Julie ran; she jumped the tufts on the grass verge, bent under the yews, cut her bare feet on the groundsel roots, was stung by the nettles.

'Where are you?'

'Here, Bernard.'

'Darling.'

'I shouldn't have come.'

'Where were you last night?'

'At the hospital, visiting someone.'

'Tell that to the marines.'

'For God's sake, don't be like that. It's true. I'll explain. But don't let's fight.'

'No, Julie.'

He led her along the road, bumping together, kissing, stopping to kiss more.

'Hup!' to the brute beast in the gateway; it lumbered off and the figure of eight wire on the upright stanchion was flicked away.

'This'll do.'

Bernard's coat pleated under them, the clay wet and lumpy, he said: 'We should have gone away this weekend, as I suggested.'

'I know. It was impossible.'

'But all this horsy stuff is ridiculous.'

'It's a job. Like any other. I had to acquit myself; leave at my own chosen speed.'

'That's jargon. And will winning prizes in this one-horse town alter your life?'

'But if we'd gone off together, we'd have been back in a couple of days. More pleasure more pain, surely?'

'You're wrong. You must do what you want to do when you want to do it; you'll never want to do it in the same way again.'

'I made a mistake,' Julie said. 'But it's too late.'

'Yes, it's too late now. And tomorrow, or the next day, I may stop loving you and you may stop loving me; our relationship will tail off in a wishy-washy way.'

'Do you want it to end?'

'That's not what I said at all.'

'When can I see you again?'

Bernard looked down at me, laughed. 'You know where I live,' he said.

'Don't ever let me go, say you won't.'

Bernard laughed again. 'Why should I do that,' he said. 'As long as you're around, I'll see you. Cheer up.'

We went out on to the road.

'There's too much tragedy around,' he said. 'Don't you remember when you wrote "Bernard's daft" on the undercoating? When I was painting the walls?'

'That was before Rose came.'

'Rose, Rose, Rose.'

Bernard's daft. I began a mad laugh.

I hate histrionics; all my life I've tried to avoid hysterical girls.

So Nicholas said.

A masochistic orgy.

'Bernard's daft,' I shouted.

'Shh,' he said, trying to keep his patience. 'Brennen might pass.'

'The neighbours,' I screamed. 'Petit bourgeois suburbia, lace curtains. You and your precious Rose's reputation. You don't give a damn about me. Say it . . . say it . . . '

I began to sing at the top of my voice:

> Rose Rose Rose Rose,
> Shall I ever see thee wed,
> Aye, marry, that I will,
> When thou art dead . . .

'For Christ's sake.'

My screams were not relevant to his life, only to mine. I raved on and on. He held me as firmly as he could. Then suddenly he lost his temper and slapped me on the face.

'Shut up!'

Astonished, I stopped immediately. 'I'm sorry. I'm very sorry.'

'So you should be.'

He led me back to my bicycle.

## 31

The day of the Girvan show dawned, as it had to dawn, even if all the protagonists had died overnight. And we'd arranged to compromise, O'Hagan and myself. By devious method, I had persuaded him to accept the ride in the Hunter Trials on Bella while I rode her in the open championship; flirting with him, pretending acquiescence in future, and no doubt in general teasing and accentuating his agony. And all the time, my own agony was my own lump that I must take to the show and bring back, whether or not I rode in the championship, whether or not I fell and broke my neck.

It was drizzling. It always drizzled at the Girvan show, they said. It was an old-style country show. Tea and bar by courtesy of Mrs Lawlor of Naas. Lemonade from O'Hagan. Whiskey from myself and Des Mooney. Mrs Travers in heather-mixture suit, canvas boots, and shooting-stick pork-pie hat with pheasant's feather attached, could all have been hired from Moss Bros, like it said in *Country Life*. She bestowed smiles on the greater and lesser gentry, the lesser tradespeople, the professionals, as pigs in the middle, the doctor, the vet, the solicitor, the bank manager, Mrs Howard (the chemist's wife – nearly a professional – and instigator of the minor cultural scene), the bishop, his son, who barely nodded, the odious Brennen in Sunday best, worn and shiny at the arse, the eldest son, the original voyeur, with his hair steamed down on his forehead and shining pink face. I hated so much at that moment his pious little face like a registered angel. An angel of hell, and Girvan, and Lady G. herself, presiding with withdrawn dignity at the veg stall, selling or judging prize marrows; dogs barking; tinker children opportuning, 'A little help, for me and the babby', 'the blessings of', and the horses kicking and swishing their tails a whinnying, roulette and *Find the Lady*.

Poverty, quality and sometimes eccentricity, but never a friendly face.

I tightened Bella's girth, vaulted on to her and shortened my stirrup a notch.

Well out of view of Mrs Travers, I waited for the steward to flag me on.

The previous horse had scattered the stone wall, incurring four faults; the best round to date.

Lackeys of the establishment were rebuilding it. I waited till they'd finished and the photographers had resettled, then I cantered briskly into the ring.

There was a shout from somewhere and a figure burst out from the crowd; I went once round the steward. O'Hagan, his bullying face red, tried to catch the mare's reins. I kicked her into a gallop, sliding away from him, and hell-bent I went into the first fence. Once she'd cleared this, I collected her; she was gathered and poised, the muscles between my knees; confidently rhythmic, she jumped perfectly.

'No faults!' The man with the loud hailer had two vents in his tweed jacket and wore a rakish trilby.

I patted Bella as we trotted into the anonymity of the crowd.

Sitting in the saddle, I watched the rest of the competition. There was only one other clear round, a big rangy chestnut from Dundalk. We jumped off.

The in-and-out railway gates and the triple bar were raised a few inches.

The chestnut was going nicely; three clear and the hooves thundering into the double, and then a second of disunity and a wild dive into the first gate threw his rider. I took my time on the bay mare; she jumped as before, faultlessly. That was that.

The show was over; people dispersed. Nobody spoke to me. I took the animal on a string and trotted the two of them through the town. Des came out of his shop to congratulate me. Looking down at his hopeful nutshell eyes, from the shunting impatient horses, I said glumly that I'd meet him later, and feeling like a bag of earth, I rode back to the castle, the exhilaration of not only winning but beating them at their own game dimmed by the thought of the evening ahead and how it might have been spent otherwise had I not been so stupid.

'I'll feel lonesome when you leave,' Des said. 'In spite of barely seeing you these last few weeks.'

I downed my drinks and cackled like a young witch with her first broomstick.

'Arrah, childe, where will I find a stand-in?'

'Put in an ad,' I said, trying to stay with him, trying not to wander into fields of vagueness, trying not to look at the door, hoping . . . for what? The pub was full of strange voices, happenings. Minor rows stopping and starting; show night was fever night, and I was carried away by the hysteria of fast drinking. All sorts of distant men made passes at the few lassies in the bar, shoving and spilling drinks, cursing and spitting. In the middle of it all, I ran out into the street, found my bike, got on and fell off. Outside, it was even worse; the street, illuminated by puddles, reflected figures of every size and shape, carts and ponies and donkeys champing with boredom, bicycles and dogs, children and very old, very drunk men; they passed my crumpled body lying in the gutter; some tripped, some stared; a hand picked me up: 'It's the young one from the castle!'

I hastened away; forged into the wind and rain and the steep incline out of town.

The band swung and banged behind the flapping canvas walls of the marquee. Brown paper parcels of stout piled up like ballast on the windward side.

'Are you coming to the dance?'

Outside, an old fiddler ripped away at his instrument; a grand-mother cracked her walnut bones.

My body swung loosely from the noise and the voluptuous banging of the canvas. Into the waltzing lash of the black wet night . . .

One, two, three . . . One, two, three . . .

'Are you coming to the dance?'

# 32

The following day, Julie de Vraie, girl of the true, jack of all trades, set off for Girvan dressed for tennis. Ha bloody ha, she thought, to hell with them. I'll pass the time if it kills me.

So she cycled, tennis racket tied crossways with a string to the handlebars. Once in the past, long ago, she'd suggested to Bernard that the two of them should play in the mixed doubles. Have you deserted your wits? What wits?

She reached the clubhouse through the marsh. *Squelch squelch* went her shoes. She entered the pavilion. There were some pundits from Dublin, an insulated group, chattering in the corner, waiting, like everyone else, for the rain to stop. She stood alone at the open veranda watching the raindrops gather, first round and then pear-shaped, till they stretched to their utmost and fell *splat* on the balustrade.

'Have you a partner for the mixed doubles?'

Julie turned: 'I'm mesmerised by the rain.'

'Aren't we all? But if it clears, will you play with me?'

Julie trapped her buttocks against the wooden struts. 'Surely,' she said.

'I'm sure you're good.'

'Why?'

'You're the right shape.'

'You must be from Dublin?'

'That's right. Trinity.'

His hair curled tightly into the nape of his neck.

'What's your name?'

'Herman.'

Jewish?

He had a Roman profile. Not Jewish?

The rain stopped.

'I knew you'd be good,' he said, as they exchanged sides with their opponents.

'Tennis is easy,' Julie said.

'What else are you good at?'

'Ah ha . . . '

'And what are you going to be when you grow up?'

Julie's lips slipped in and out between her teeth: 'Your serve!'

After one set, the brief watery sun went in and the rain came down good and proper. The rest of the tournament was cancelled and the prizes distributed to potential winners: gift tokens for Hely's of Dame Street, Dublin.

'Herman?'

'Yes?'

'Are you all going to the Majestic?'

'Aren't you coming along?'

They swung down the muddy lane: 'And I don't even know your surname!' he said.

'De Vraie.'

Herman stopped. 'Not Columbine? I've heard of her.'

'Excuse me,' Julie said. 'But the merry-go-round stops here.'

Herman shrugged; he wasn't that interested.


As Julie had finally wheeled her bicycle into the shed during the small hours of the previous night, covered in weals from a sojourn in a ditch, she had been snatched at from behind.

'You good as promised. It must be my turn.'

O'Hagan, determined this time, had torn her pants down and pushed his penis between her thighs.

But she'd squeezed away, mad, scratching her way out, her hands like briars, and screaming: 'Fuck off.'

'You bitch . . . You foul bitch . . . bitch . . . '

She trailed after them. They were soon ensconsed in the lounge of the Majestic.

'Ah,' Herman sang out. 'My partner, what'll she have?'

She prayed that the merry-go-round would grind to a halt and ordered a gin and lime.

They bought rounds, these pretty boys and girls from Dublin; plenty of money; rich mummies and daddies and a girl with a tight dark face looked at Herman all the time and Herman ignored her. He knew she was there . . . if it was handed to him on a plate! And Julie demolished much liquor in as short as possible a time and they sat or lay against the armchairs, Herman in one and Julie resting on the floor beside him, her elbow on his knee.

'We'll sing some good songs . . .

> Oh, the Garden of Eden is vanished they say,
> But I know the lie of it still . . . '

'Come on, everybody . . . sing.'

A figure entered. A stylish figure. Went up to the counter. Ordered a drink. Then turned to survey the holocaust.

'Bernard!' Julie screamed.

The expression in the grape eyes was caustic.

'Bernard,' she screamed again.

She tried to get up, half did so, stumbled, spilled her drink, fell back purposefully into Herman's arms; she pulled his head down to hers, her arched back very stiff. She kissed him, running her tongue round the inside of his cheek. She turned and shouted: 'Bernard! Come and meet my new friends from Dublin. Lovely people!'

She looked ghastly. Her hair was at its worst, scattered on all sides like wet weeds; a single shoulder strap trailed down her arm, her bare feet were tucked under her, and two holey stinking tennis shoes lay beside them on the floor. She alternatively kissed Herman and yelled: 'Bernard.'

But he had taken one look, knocked back his drink and gone.

'Herman,' Julie slavered. 'Let's go upstairs and meet my lover. He is waiting to kill me on the landing . . . Ha ha . . . ' She dragged Herman to his feet and dragged him out into the corridor ' . . . Oh Bernard . . . Bernard . . . C'mon. Herman!' They plunged up a flight and along another corridor, with Julie caterwauling and muling till Herman shoved her into a room and had her immediately against the wall. There were roses on the wallpaper.

'Roses,' Julie screamed. 'Rose, rose, rose, rose, Shall I ever see thee red, wed, dead . . . '

The room began to spin. She clutched the bed as it rushed past her. She missed it and fell sideways on her face. She clambered to her hands and knees and vomited like a dog on the floor. She retched till great splurges of drink rushed through her mouth and nose. She squatted down like an old squaw and stared at the opposite wall, her skinny frame shaking and swaying. She tried to focus on something human but Herman had gone.

There is something wrong. It's morning. Seems to be morning. Dawn had splintered in; faded the bulb into a pale yellow. Julie was on the bed. Had someone lifted her on, or had she climbed on, unaided? Hardly interesting. The artificial bedcover was fragmented underneath her. Where are your shoes? Herman . . . Bernard. Oh . . . how dreadful! God, Bernard. Had he really been there last night? What time? Why, why, why? You are still in tennis shorts. Tennis shorts smooth are bad enough . . . but tennis shorts crumpled at six . . . seven . . . eight . . . are highly improbable.

She got up, staggered, fumbled with the door handle. Water . . . water . . .

The army is closing in. Water!

She tottered into the fusty corridor of this alien hotel. Its carpeted length fondled her bare feet. She surreptitiously opened doors. Forms slumbered. Leisure. That's what it is. Leisure to feel, to think, to act with forethought. Never made a mistake. These bodies make no mistakes. They sleep in organised fashion, their beds paid for in advance. They never sleep in their clothes or do anything that might cost them something afterwards. Caution. Sensible caution displayed while they nevertheless enjoy themselves. How do they do it?

And there was Herman, bronze hair and all. All on the pillow, comfortably asleep in spick-and-span surroundings; a reclining Nero before and after. She went to his bed, shook him, said: 'Wake up!'

Herman moaned and turned away.

She climbed in beside him and without opening his eyes he rolled on top of her and, in a second or two, rolled away. Julie jumped up and ran to the lavatory.

They say if you piss immediately afterwards, you're safe.

Old wives' tales?

Who is this person, shivering on the porcelain, sitting there with her elbows on her knees? What is she doing?


And the lounge is dark downstairs, shut in with its smell of stale tobacco, and the carpet is stained with beer; residual stains trail from the necks of bottles like blood.

Why don't you turn on the light and get your shoes.

There they are. You must put them on. Get your feet into them. Don't undo the laces. Get out. Out. Into the sleeping town. Your bicycle . . . your bicycle.

You must pedal hard now. No loitering. Hurry up. Faster, faster. Don't slow down there. He won't come down that turn now and you won't go up it either. Will you?

Do you hear the corncrake?

## OTHER TITLES BY LELAND BARDWELL

### AUTOBIOGRAPHY
*A Restless Life*. Dublin, Liberties Press, 2008.

### NOVELS
*Girl on a Bicycle*. Dublin, Irish Writers Co-operative, 1977.
*That London Winter*. Dublin, Co-op Books, 1981.
*The House*. Dingle, Brandon Books, 1984.
*There We Have Been*. Dublin, Attic Press, 1989.
*Mother to a Stranger*. Belfast, The Blackstaff Press, 2002. (German
    edition, *Mutter Eines Fremden*, translated Hans-Christian Oeser,
    published Verlag C. H. Beck, 2004)

### SHORT STORIES
*Different Kinds of Love*. Dublin, Attic Press, 1987.

### POETRY
*The Mad Cyclist*. Dublin, New Writers' Press, 1970.
*The Fly and the Bed Bug*. Dublin, Beaver Row Press, 1984.
*Dostoevsky's Grave: Selected Poems*. Dublin, Dedalus Press, 1991.
*The White Beach: New and Selected Poems, 1960-1998*. Cliffs of Moher,
    Salmon Publishing, 1998.
*The Noise of Masonry Settling*. Dublin, Dedalus Press, 2006.

## PLAYS

*Thursday.* Dublin, Trinity College, 1972.
*Open Ended Prescription.* Dublin, Peacock Theatre, 1979.
*Edith Piaf.* Dublin, Olympia Theatre, 1984.
*Jocasta.* Sligo, Hawk's Well Theatre Company, 2000.

## OTHER

Founder editor, *Cyphers*, 1975–2008.
Contributor, *Ms Muffet and Others: A Funny, Sassy, Heretical Collection of Feminist Fairytales.* Dublin, Attic Press, 1986.
Editor, with others, *The Anthology.* Dublin, Co-op Books, 1982.

## SELECTED TRANSLATIONS

*Mutter Eines Fremden,* translated Hans-Christian Oeser, published Verlag C. H. Beck, 2004.
With Anthony Cronin and Paul Durcan, *Literatura irlandzka, tom drugi: w tlumaczeniu na język polski.* Poznan, Motivex, 2003.

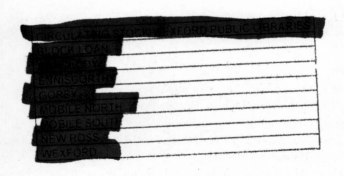